THE FATAL DARK

FINAL DAWN ☀ BOOK NINE

T.W.M. ASHFORD

DARK STAR PANORAMA

The *Dark Star Panorama* is a shared universe of sci-fi stories in which *Final Dawn* is the first series.

To hear about new releases and receive an exclusive, free prequel story set in the *Final Dawn* series, sign up for T.W.M. Ashford's mailing list at the website below.

www.twmashford.com

THE FATAL DARK

1

SIMA-TET

S ima-Tet sprinted back inside her hut and slammed the door behind her. The man to whom she had been spirit-bonded for fourteen cycles was dead. Her mother was dead also, reduced to a mist before Sima-Tet's eyes. All that remained of her family was her infant son, dozing in his crib. She wrapped him tightly in his nursing-cloth and bundled him into her arms.

Only a few weeks old, Lume-Tet's only experience of the world was that of slumber and lullabies. For half a cycle this should have remained so, unseen save by the eyes of mother and father, to keep from forever cursing the boy with ill fortune. This was the Ellinian way, never to be broken. But she wouldn't let tradition rob her only child of his elder years.

Besides, his life was already unfortunate enough.

Sima-Tet went to grab food, coins, heirlooms, then thought better of it. There wasn't time, nor had she the arms to carry more than Lume-Tet anyway. If they made it off Ellini alive, they would have to rely on the kindness of strangers to survive. Everything truly valuable in her life – aside from her son, of course – was already gone.

She hurried out of the hut's living quarters and into a bedroom whose walls were flush with shawls. Barging through the rear door with her shoulder, Sima-Tet instinctively closed it again behind her. It was unnecessary – any Ellinian stupid enough to stop and loot empty homes wasn't likely to live long enough to enjoy the spoils.

Despite all the evidence, Sima-Tet couldn't bring herself to believe she was actually saying goodbye.

An explosion nearby made her shriek and flinch back inside the doorway. The city before her was in a better state than that which lay behind, but only just. Whole neighbourhoods of huts were on fire, their thatched roofs burning like funeral pyres. Old Turrim, a tower which had survived five hundred years and three entire dynasties of rule, lay crumbled in the streets. The heavens were the colour of rage and jealousy, plagued by black ships that resembled primeval bugs.

Why would anyone attack us? she wondered desperately, wishing she could collapse to the floor and cry. *We have little enough as it is.*

Sima-Tet edged around the outer wall of her hut and peered back down the street from which she came. Too far back and all she could see was smoke and the crackle of weaponry she couldn't conjure in even her darkest nightmares. From out of that obfuscated slaughter poured a stream of distraught townsfolk.

She recognised one of her neighbours, quickly grabbed his arm as he passed her by.

"What's happening, Balla-Gup? Where is everybody going?"

"Evacuation," her neighbour replied, shaking off her

hand as he disappeared back into the screaming crowd. "Shuttles by the—"

Sima-Tet never caught his final words, so loud were the cries of the survivors around her. She supposed it didn't matter. Everyone was headed in the same direction with the same purpose in their heart – safe passage off Ellini. All she needed to do was follow the tide.

Clutching Lume-Tet to her chest, patting the back of his head gently as he began to cry, she merged with the flow of survivors sprinting down the street. Immediately she felt the emaciated elbows of others digging into her sides like spears, shoves from yesterday's friends behind, clumsy feet tripping over her own. Dust blew into her eyes and mouth until she was unable to see more than a few Ellinians in front of her or breathe without her lungs setting ablaze.

Ellini was not a rich nation. They had no imperial fleet with which to defend themselves – their greatest defence had always been not having anything worth stealing. Most citizens of that small, forgotten planet could scarcely afford to travel to the next city over, let alone the stars. Shuttles off-world would be few.

Sima-Tet wished she weren't so terribly aware of this truth.

"So long as you are safe," she whispered to Lume-Tet. She tried to cover his wailing mouth with a fold of his nursing-cloth to keep him from swallowing the same grit she did. "So long as you are safe..."

She raised her head to find a haggard man bolting back the opposite way.

"Blocked," he screamed at her, his eyes streaming. "The street is blocked, hear me? They've—"

Suddenly he was gone, transformed into a static-electric cloud of vapour in the same manner as her mother mere minutes before. Sima-Tet gasped and fell backwards into a produce stall. Baskets of bread and fruit tumbled over her and Lume-Tet in a landslide.

Something stalked through the dust storm. Sima-Tet's breath caught in her throat. She instinctively pressed her son tighter against her chest, both to protect him and stifle his cries.

The creature stopped three feet from where she lay blanketed by spoiled foods. It raised its black, carapaced head as if sensing her presence. Peeking out at it, Sima-Tet was horrified to witness a craggy exoskeleton that looked older than even the Tangum Hills and a pair of eyes as red as a branding iron.

It took another clawed step towards her.

But then more unfortunate Ellinians came running into the open, and the bloodthirsty monster quickly resumed its hunt. The second it left her sight, Sima-Tet climbed out of the market wreckage and ducked into the nearest alley peeling off the main road.

"Please take breath," she said, desperately peeling back layers of nursing-cloth. "Please take breath..."

Lume-Tet began to wail again. She smiled in mournful relief, then reapplied the folds.

"Gods, I miss you, Jekka-Tet." A single tear ran down her lime cheek as she ignored the sounds of war closing in around her. "You would know what to do."

But so do you, she told herself. *You may not know where you're headed, but you know what to look for.*

Everybody had been following the road south before the invader cut them down. Her best bet was to keep heading in that same direction, only off the beaten path.

And if she came across a shuttle – no, *when* she came

across a shuttle – she would take it... or die getting Lume-Tet on board.

Hunching her shoulders and bowing her head against the waves of smoke drifting between the huts, Sima-Tet charged through the cracks and alleyways. New ships screamed overhead, chased by or chasing the flying fossils in which the invaders arrived. Friend or foe, she didn't recognise these either.

She paused when she came to a crossing, hid behind a flapping, sun-scorched banner as another pair of hulking ancient monsters marched past. One flicked its clawed hand disdainfully, splashing a spatter of blood across the sandy road. The other carried one of the guns used to kill Sima-Tet's family. To her, it looked like a petrified tree branch; she had never in her life seen anything so ghastly.

The way ahead clear, she crossed to the next alley over. Bodies lay sprawled out in the dirt, their eyes glazed and stomachs torn open. Sima-Tet pressed her son even closer to her chest as she stepped carefully over them. This was an unthinkable sight for any child, let alone one expected to see only his own parents for his first half-cycle.

She passed others as she hurried through the back streets – parents crying over their lost children, younglings wandering the deserted huts, confused, and the elderly who were too frail to flee. She could not risk helping them, though she wished in her heart she could. To stop was to die, she'd seen that. Saving Lume-Tet was now all that mattered.

With sudden clarity, Sima-Tet realised where she was heading – Yelbez Square. Most of their city was crowded with huts of stone and straw, and even some of the streets had become lost over the decades as their population expanded.

But the Square was an untouchable presence in Ellinian society. Many of the ruling houses had spoken to their subjects from its pulpit over the centuries – almost as many as there'd been subjects who hanged for raising arms against them. If there was anywhere better to safely land a transport shuttle this side of the mountains, Sima-Tet didn't know it.

It wasn't far.

She raced forwards, barely keeping an eye on where she was going for fear of what she might encounter, stumbling more than once on the higgledy steps and discarded baskets in her way. She bashed into another survivor bursting out from between an outhouse and a well, knocked her into the dirt, and apologised pleadingly without slowing.

Her two hearts fell. A thick plume of dark grey smoke belched up from a few lanes over where she knew the Square to be. Whatever had been brought there was surely destroyed. But she had to know for sure.

Emerging into the Square from behind an upturned cart, her fears proved correct. One of the ships above had crashed into the sand-swept clearing and exploded upon impact. Flames so hot they singed the hairs on Sima-Tet's arms still roared inside the buckled fuselage. The sliding doors were open. Burned Ellinian bodies hung out of the sides as if still trying to escape the blaze.

Sima-Tet turned, came close to throwing up. Lume-Tet began to cry again. She rocked him and stepped away from the wreckage and its heat. She would have cried herself had she the energy left.

"You!" came a hoarse voice from the other side of the derelict Square. "You there, *shemiken*. Are you coming?"

Now Sima-Tet *did* cry, and a hopeful smile dared flicker across her face. A second transport shuttle was parked opposite her, its thrusters blaring like twin suns. Its carriage was packed full of Ellinian refugees. A Jakkashi guard stood half-out the door, a plasma rifle in hand. Their kind belonged to a neighbouring star system yet she'd never seen one outside of a holo-stream before.

"We've got to go!" the guard shouted, beckoning her over. "You need to leave now!"

The shriek of laser fire in the neighbouring streets booted her free from her stupor. Sima-Tet sprinted for the shuttle, her bundle shaking in her arms, certain her rescuers would suffer the same fate as the other transporter before she got there. The Jakkashi pulled her sharply into the vehicle as soon as she came within his reach.

"Take her up!" the guard barked at a pilot Sima-Tet couldn't see.

The shuttle shot upwards. She whimpered and grasped the nearest rail with her free hand. The shuttle doors weren't even closed yet. With so many Ellinians crammed on board, Sima-Tet couldn't see how they ever would. Never had she been so high before; already the grand towers and rambling neighbourhoods of the only city she had ever known were as small as the babe cradled in her arms.

"We have incoming," the Jakkashi guard shouted, pointing his rifle out of the open doors beside her. "Brace!"

Sima-Tet stared in open-mouthed horror as one of the ancient ships raced after them. They looked like pesky black bugs from down on the ground; up here, they morphed into the spiny dragons of legend. Those inside the shuttle shut their eyes and held their loved ones tight.

Then, with a rumble like that of a gored boar, a Jakkashi gunship tore into the invader's vessel with a stream of thunderous ballistic rounds. Their pursuer – which Sima-Tet was certain had to be alive, no machine she knew could writhe in such a pained manner – splintered apart and fell from the sky. The Jakkashi gunship swept past their shuttle with zero ceremony, and once more Sima-Tet shrank back, questioning who to fear most.

The guard punched the wall separating the fuselage from the cockpit twice.

"Up and out," he grunted.

The sliding doors shot along their tracks and locked shut. Everybody inside was trapped shoulder to shoulder, cheek to cheek. Sima-Tet had to push somebody away from her just to check if Lume-Tet still took breath; *she* surely couldn't.

The shuttle rattled as it picked up speed, increased its angle of ascent. Its occupants all took a pained step backwards. Lume-Tet screamed; another child of no more than four years began to bawl. The pressure on Sima-Tet's ribcage was so great, she couldn't even comfort her son. She didn't understand. It felt as if she were falling back through her world, not away from it.

Fighting to maintain her balance as the alien shuttle shook so violently it was sure to tear itself apart, she brought the trembling bundle that was her child up to her face, muttered soothing melodies, and began to pray.

To give thanks for all she saved.

To mourn all she had lost.

To bid farewell to all that she called home, for neither she nor her son would ever see Ellini again.

2

NOTHING RANDOM

The *Adeona* tore through Kondath's methane-heavy atmosphere and punched a hole into subspace. Her crew gathered around the hologram table in her cockpit, sifting through the frenzy of incoming reports.

"The Krolaks have negotiated a ceasefire with the Alpha Rhoden, thanks to the Prymalis firebombing their home-world, Kiratho." Jack swatted at one news item so he could read it better on his data pad. "That's something to be thankful for, I guess…"

"Remember those salt mines the Qetho Zsar extremists liberated from hard working belt miners?" Rogan said. "Gone. Vaporised – and three quarters of the Qetho Zsar clan vaporised along with them. Not the galaxy's worst loss, mind you, but it demonstrates the ruthlessness with which the Prymalis will dispatch any resource that outlives its usefulness."

"How are the Krolaks holding out?" Tuner asked. "They've got one of the biggest fleets after the Mansa Empire."

"Kiratho isn't as bad as once feared," Jack said, scrolling down. "Tens of thousands dead, as many as a million displaced. So, you know, pretty damn bad. But their fleet was on high alert thanks to existing tensions with the Alpha Rhoden, so they knew something was coming. They took significant losses but managed to destroy all three Prymalis battleships."

"And now there's no question that the ancients are the ones wreaking havoc across the galaxy," Rogan added. "All the major empires have got the ruins to prove it. Maybe now they'll stop fighting amongst themselves and focus on fighting the real enemy."

"Shame we don't have the right weapon to fight them with," Jack muttered bitterly under his breath.

The *Adeona* was inside of a week back from a two-month trip outside of the known galaxy to an extroplanet designated XO-R15. En route, they'd discovered Tectus Maximilian's derelict frigate from his own voyage almost nine hundred years earlier and salvaged what appeared to be a bomb from its cargo hold. Taking it to an AI arms dealer called A.M.I. on Kondath had illuminated its purpose – to mass-deliver a neurotoxin that could render the whole Prymalis race extinct – but also its newfound redundancy. It had been designed for deployment inside XO-R15's atmosphere. With the enormous enemy fleet now spread so widely across the galaxy, it was impossible for the payload to have even a fraction of its intended effectiveness. Max's mysterious device had turned out to be no more useful to the war effort than a two-tonne paperweight.

Extrapolating from all the battles waged against the ancients thus far, it took approximately half a dozen battlecruisers to take down a single Prymalis warship. Even with every major military power working together, they still might not have the numbers to beat such a colossal force. It was simple maths. Even Jack could see that.

But they had to keep fighting, no matter the cost. The alternative was complete galactic annihilation. As hopeless as it got, there was simply no other choice.

"Oh no," said Tuner, highlighting a fresh report. "This one's particularly bad…"

Rogan enlarged the report on the hologram table, but while the two automata could, in essence, download it directly, the details were still too grainy for Jack to read without giving himself a migraine.

"Adi, is it all right if we beam this onto the cockpit windows instead?"

"Of course," the ship replied. "It's not as if we've got much of a view to look at, anyway…"

Amongst the pulsing blue-black void outside the ship lay a lone speck of blinding white light. It was soon blocked out by a rapidly expanding portfolio of documents and video feeds.

Rogan bowed her head. Tuner waddled from one paddle-foot to the other while wringing his small metal digits together.

"What am I looking at?" Jack asked uneasily. From the automata's reactions, he guessed he didn't want to know.

"This is Crysarri Prime," Tuner replied. "Or it was, at any rate. It's an Oort cloud, though not the one orbiting your old star system. That's the environment in which the original Oortilians evolved. They tend to base their colonies there."

"Oort Clouds." Jack chewed his bottom lip. "They're sort of like belts of icy asteroids, right? Are they, erm, supposed to look like that?"

"Like that?" Rogan pointed at one of the video screens.

"No. That's not a feed of the whole cloud, Jack. That debris is what's left of their capital city."

"Ah. That is particularly bad, then."

Jack watched with a lead stomach as the video zoomed in to reveal the full extent of the damage. Oort clouds consisted of thousands of habitable planetesimals, some large enough to establish entire cities on. Crysarri Prime was an example of this, the metropolis occupying every inch of its asteroid-sized surface. But the objects in Oort clouds are predominantly made of ice given their terrific distance from any sun. Fine for a native Oortilian in peacetime; terrible when somebody turned up holding a big enough gun.

Crysarri Prime was shattered, as were its closest neighbouring settlements. Chunks of glistening terrain and industrial cityscapes drifted morbidly through the black ether.

"How many dead?" Jack asked with a sigh.

"Estimates are as high as one point two million," Rogan replied. "It happened too quickly for anyone to issue an evacuation, though I understand some of its population managed to escape in their ships even after the colony cracked apart."

"Jesus Christ. That's terrible."

"Here's a name you'll recognise amongst the dead, too." Rogan highlighted a passage in one of the written reports. "Grand Minister Heram. He was reportedly visiting Crysarri Prime to discuss Oortilian relief measures following the disbandment of the Ministerium."

"Oh my—" Jack shook his head. "That's horrible. We spoke to him only a few days ago! Come on. The galactic community *has* to do something now!"

"You'd think that." Rogan shrugged. "Tens of millions are surely dead already. And that's just from the major attacks getting reported. The figure is probably far higher than that because most of the smaller planets aren't getting as much extranet time. Grand Minister Heram may have been an important political figure once, but the Ministry is effectively over once the relief fund runs dry. Now he's nothing but another statistic. Just because we knew him – if you can even say we did – doesn't make his death any more important than anyone else's."

"Oh, come on. He was a *Grand Minister,* Rogan. Are you seriously suggesting the Oortilians won't want justice for this?"

"Yes, of course they will. And they'll try to get it by attacking the Prymalis the first chance they get, the same as everyone else who's lost mayors and cities and planets over the past week. Just because the Oortilians want justice for Heram doesn't mean the Mansa or the Krolaks care enough to join them."

"With that attitude," Tuner said, slumping onto a chair with his cassette-shaped head in his hands, "we'll never win."

"Don't blame me," Rogan said apologetically. "It's only thanks to the four of us that anyone's even trying to fix this mess."

"Not that we seem to be having much success," the *Adeona* said, somehow infusing even that despondent sentence with her usual dose of cheerfulness. "I don't even know where I'm supposed to be headed right now."

"I dare say it doesn't matter," Jack grunted. "The Prymalis will find us no matter where we go."

They were all out of leads. Travelling to XO-R15 had

shed light on who was attacking the galaxy and why, but achieved little in figuring out a way stop them. Max's bomb was a dead end – they'd left it behind on Kondath for A.M.I. to tinker with. Anyone friendly who might know a way to win the war was dead, and their enemy hardly possessed the civil disposition (or intelligence, in the case of the Rakletts) to sit down and chat.

And the longer Jack and the crew of the *Adeona* spent figuring out what their next step was, the further into the galaxy the Prymalis battleships crept.

Jack had been drumming his fingers against the cockpit dashboard. Now his index finger hovered mid-beat.

The further into the galaxy the Prymalis battleships crept.

"Rogan," he said, spinning around. "How quickly can you put together a map of where all the reported Prymalis attacks have taken place?"

"Give me a minute," she said, typing away. "There," she added less than thirty seconds later. "Every confirmed Prymalis attack since Paryx got glassed. I've highlighted the unconfirmed reports in yellow, just in case."

Jack took a deep breath. Apparently there were even more sites than he knew about. Some he recognised, others belonged to systems so out of the way he could have easily gone a lifetime without learning their names.

"Do you want them highlighted in order of when the attacks took place?" Rogan asked, moving to input the command.

"No, that's okay," Jack said quickly. "It's the full picture we need to be studying. Maybe what looks like a series of random attacks isn't actually random at all."

Tuner climbed up on the terminal beside them for a better look.

"So Paryx was first," he said, pointing at the corresponding blip on the galaxy map. "And then Yanna Lös came next, as far as we know."

"Both systems are in the same quadrant," Rogan said cautiously, "but on completely opposite sides from one another."

"We know that the Prymalis travel via the old subspace routes they forged," Jack explained, "yet Barataria was left completely alone. That would have been the first populated planet they came across, right? Maybe they ignored it because the ancients don't fear a bunch of pirate clans who can hardly go a day without warring amongst themselves..."

"Or maybe they're deliberately hiding where they started," Rogan said, catching on.

"And with that," Jack said hopefully, "where they plan to *finish*."

"Do we have a lead?" Tuner asked excitedly. "It sounds like we have a lead!"

"Don't blow a fuse just yet," Jack said. He couldn't help smiling, though – Tuner's enthusiasm was contagious. "It's just an idea. And my ideas usually aren't very smart."

"I don't know, Jack." Rogan pondered the map. "You might be on to something. On the face of it, there doesn't seem to be any pattern to the attacks. First they strike here, then a different set of battleships appears over here hours later. The majority of incidents are occurring across the same two quadrants, but anomalous attacks have also been reported far on the other side of the galaxy. It's impossible to predict where the Prymalis will appear next. Yet, taken as a whole, it seems clear to me that their overall path is slowly tapering towards a central point, no matter how hard they try to mask it. Everybody's been in too great a panic to stop and notice."

They all peered at the blip Rogan was pointing at. It

wasn't the actual centre of the galaxy, of course. That was Sagittarius A, a black hole with four million times the mass of Sol. If only they were so lucky as for the Prymalis to pilot themselves into *that*.

"They're headed for Kapamentis," Jack said. The words felt numb in his mouth.

"The Ministerium, the Libraries." Rogan nodded. "The Prymalis have a lot of history there. It makes sense they'd want it back."

"But it's also the most densely populated metropolis in the whole galaxy," Tuner said. "We've got to do something!"

"Like what?" Jack asked. "Rock up outside Kapamentis with a giant megaphone and tell everyone to leg it?"

"The best we can do is pass this information along to somebody with the power to issue an evacuation or establish a military blockade," Rogan replied. "That would have been the Grand Ministers up until a few days ago. Whose comm details do we have?"

Jack handed her his data pad. The same information was stored inside Adi, but he didn't want to lose the diagram they had up on the hologram table.

"Okay," Rogan said, scrolling through the list. "So, Philo Na Ji is with Klik on Salyn One. As far as the Mansa Empire is concerned, nothing has changed since the attack on Paryx. As amenable as Philo might be, I'm not sure what good trying to convince him to unite the Ministry races will do."

"And Grand Minister Heram is dead," Jack said flippantly, "so I doubt he's got much political sway anymore either."

"Grand Minister Zsal?" Tuner suggested. "I know she's pretty scary and all, but she's always seemed level-headed. And definitely a big supporter of a united galaxy."

"Unofficially the grandest of the Grand Ministers, too," Rogan said. "But she's got enough to deal with right now. Her homeworld is currently under heavy Prymalis bombardment. She won't want to talk to us."

"What about the other Grand Ministers?" Tuner asked. "The one who looks like a spiky explosion of black goop, or the rocky cephalopod, or—?"

"I don't even know their names," Jack said, laughing nervously. "I certainly don't have their private comm details."

"Those three were the quickest to leave the Ministry when member species started quitting," Rogan said. "They probably wouldn't care to listen to us, anyway."

They all fell silent as they thought of literally anybody else in the galaxy they could call.

"So it's Grand Minister Zsal, then." Jack sighed. "I bet she's gonna be real glad to hear from us again."

"The perpetual pain in her backside," Rogan mused. "But, you know. I'm sure news of an impending assault on Kapamentis will really brighten up her day."

"Maybe she's getting bored only looking after her own species," Tuner suggested sheepishly. "She always used to like bossing the others about."

"Adi," Jack said to the speakers, "are you able to drop out of subspace for a moment? We need to make a call."

"Skipping back into the middle of nowhere in three... two... one..."

They burst into Dark Space – the anonymous cosmic void between star systems. If only he didn't need to eat food, Jack thought to himself. A ship could float out there for millennia without the Prymalis ever finding them.

Well, there was an idea for the galaxy's continued survival. Billions of isolated ships, lightyears away from one another, forever hiding out of sight. Maybe he could start growing potatoes and peas in the *Adeona's* pantry.

"Grand Minister Zsal's comm channel is ready," the ship announced. "Would you like me to connect the call?"

Jack braced himself. Speaking to Zsal always made him feel as if he were about to receive a telling off, even when he was delivering *good* news. Admittedly, that hadn't been often.

"Yes please, Adi."

They waited wordlessly. Tuner nervously drummed his feet against the side of his terminal.

"—who—who is this?" came a crackling, distorted voice as their call connected. It sort of sounded like Zsal, but the audio quality was too poor to tell for sure.

"It's Jack Bishop," he said, shouting as if the technical problems were at his end. Rogan shook her head. "And the crew of the *Ad*—"

"Jack Bishop?" replied the incredulous voice. "Why in the galaxy are *you* calling—" Something explosive went off and a wave of static flooded the comms. "Don't you—how dangerous—"

"You're breaking up, Grand Minister," Jack said. "We have extremely important information for you. The Prymalis, we think they're headed for—"

"They're *here!*" the Grand Minister snapped. "I don't have—this isn't—find someone—"

The comm channel went dead. Whether Zsal had hung up on them or their line was severed by another explosion was anyone's guess.

"She sounded like she was on the front line," Tuner murmured.

"What she sounded," Jack replied, "was even more

annoyed to hear from us than usual. Things must be pretty bad on her homeworld."

"Things are bad everywhere," Rogan said. "Everybody focussing solely on their own problems is precisely what the Prymalis want."

"Maybe we should pay her a visit in person," Jack suggested.

Rogan paused at the hologram table.

"You want us to fly into an active war zone against an enemy we can't possibly defeat, just to deliver a message the recipient didn't want to hear over comms?"

"Yes."

"Why?"

"Because she *needs* to hear it. Zsal's one of the only people who can get a message out to every other species in the Ministry. By risking our four lives today, we might save billions of lives on Kapamentis tomorrow."

"Can't argue with those maths," Tuner said, hopping down from his terminal. "Besides, like you said – things are bad *everywhere*. We can't spend the rest of the war running from disaster to disaster trying to put out fires. Especially not with what we know now."

Rogan mulled this over.

"Yes, I suppose you're right. Still, I'll send all of this data back to Detri before we go. If something happens to us, they can spread the word in our stead."

"Perfect." Jack clapped his hands together. "Can we trace the Grand Minister's location from the call? The quicker we can get in and out of that place, the better."

"I should be able to pinpoint an approximate position," Adi replied. "Plotting a course for Vekemorte now."

"It'll take us a few hours to reach it." Rogan gestured towards Jack's quarters. "You're going to want to check you haven't any leaks in that spacesuit of yours, by the way. And, well, you might want to brace yourself for the Nárva."

Jack froze in the cockpit doorway.

"Brace myself? For what? What could possibly be more daunting than a Prymalis invasion?"

Rogan raised her mechanical eyebrows.

"Let's just say you're in for a culture shock."

3

VEKEMORTE

The moment the *Adeona* skipped into orbit around Vekemorte, Jack wanted to leave it.

Dozens of destroyers and frigates and cruisers battered each other above the murky planet. He'd never seen so many Prymalis warships in one place before – not since they departed XO-RI5, at least. The battle was incomprehensible from the safe distance at which the *Adeona* drifted to a stop. Fission lasers danced in a deadly light show, ballistic rounds sprayed out like sparks from an axle grinder, and nuclear torpedoes exploded like roses in bloom.

More than half the ships belonged to the world in question and were gnarly, black grotesqueries ribbed from bow to stern with jagged bands of bone-white. Scans indicated another fleet fought a smaller contingency of Prymalis warships on the opposite side of Vekemorte. It wasn't clear who was winning.

But it wasn't even the scenes of mutual annihilation that put Jack off. There was something about the grey-green planet itself that filled his stomach with dread, something he couldn't quite put his finger on...

"The planet's pretty big," Jack said, tearing his gaze from it. Twice the size of Earth, in fact. "They can't be fighting over every square inch of it. Is there a safe route down into Vekemorte's atmosphere?"

"Safe is a somewhat relative term," Rogan replied as she studied Adi's scans of the area, "and Grand Minister Zsal will almost certainly be operating out of someplace dangerous. But we can approach the atmosphere where the dogfighting is quietest and then attempt to rendezvous with her once we're under the radar, so to speak."

"I suggest we make our descent over the Valleys of Cykyrus," Adi said. "There's a notable uptick of refugee traffic in that region, suggesting limited Prymalis activity."

"Good idea," Jack said. "You're in charge, Adi. Take us down however you see fit."

They gave the battle as wide a berth as possible, circumnavigating Vekemorte at such a distance that, without the use of telescopic video feeds, the skirmishes themselves were invisible to the naked eye. Only the planet could be seen, a giant marble of pea-green soup. By the time they reached position above Adi's designated point of entry, one of the Nárva destroyers had suffered a fatal breach and a Prymalis battleship seemed to have lost the use of its propulsion system.

"Down we go," said the *Adeona* as she plummeted towards the heliosphere.

As expected, they passed plenty of ships fleeing the other way. Most were small, personal vessels – family skiffs, corporate cruisers, a few planet-hoppers barely bigger than an escape pod and surely only fitted with the most basic of skip drives. There were some industrial frigates and freighters making their escape, too. More than once somebody tried reaching out over comms to tell the *Adeona* she was headed the wrong way.

Jack hunkered down in his captain's chair. The larger Vekemorte grew to dominate the cockpit windows, the more he suffered a horrible sinking feeling. There was a sense of darkness, of deep sickness, of *oppression* eking out from this world. The spiritual antithesis of survival and wellbeing, at least as far as Jack's gut was concerned.

Hey, he'd seen all sorts in his year or so traipsing around the galaxy. Insects, fish, bird people. Giant mech falcons and cosmic conspiracy nutjobs. Yes, Rogan had told him to brace for a culture shock... but he didn't see how the Nárva could be too far removed from the insane menagerie of species he'd already encountered.

Right?

It wasn't as if he hadn't met one of their kind before...

He gripped the arms of his chair and ignored the suffocating aura of doom closing around him like a fist.

The *Adeona* shook as she passed through the upper thermosphere and again, more violently this time, as she heated up upon entry to the mesosphere. This wasn't in itself unusual – atmospheric entry almost always came with a few lumps and bumps – but there was a real density to this transition, like diving through the air only to hit a wall of treacle. The turbulence didn't cease until they were far inside the troposphere, the final dozen kilometres above the planetary surface where even terrestrial airplanes travelled back on Earth. Still, Rogan didn't appear concerned. Jack supposed that meant he shouldn't worry, either.

What he couldn't so easily ignore was the colour palette outside the windows. He'd assumed that the planet's sickly complexion as seen from orbit was an atmospheric anomaly

– yes, Mars was almost as coppery-red on the ground as it was when viewed from space, but that's because Mars had lost its atmosphere. What you saw was what you got. But this wasn't some weird trick of refracted light, no planet-wide aurora. Everything was cursed by the same viridescent filter. The air, the clouds, the land – all of it.

Jack rose from his seat as the ship passed by the first of many contorted cliff faces, over fathomless black gulches and sweeping plains of cold desolation. Suddenly, it hit him. Green Hell – that's how Dante would have described this world. That's why he felt so uneasy. A bright flash went off on the horizon – it could have been lightning, or just as possibly an orbital strike from the Prymalis fighting above.

"Holy mother of... What *is* this place?"

"Welcome to Vekemorte," Rogan said dramatically, "the most inhospitable planet to ever spawn intelligent life."

"You mean it looked like this *before* the Prymalis turned up?"

"Be careful what you say around the Nárva," Rogan replied. "For all that they acknowledge its difficulties, they're very proud of their homeworld. It's rather unique. It also just happens to be the opposite of what most organics would expect. Vekemorte is still something of a mystery."

"But it's like an irradiated wasteland!" Jack said. "How did one of the most powerful species in the Ministerium originate from this?"

"An irradiated wasteland would be more conducive for the proliferation of life than Vekemorte's atmosphere," Rogan said, scoffing. "If you took one step outside this ship without your suit on, your skin would welt and blister and slip right off your bones. It's not the heat, nor a lack of it. The air itself is toxic to humans, as indeed it is to every known species in the galaxy save for those that first evolved here. Your lungs would dissolve the instant you took a breath. But take comfort in the knowledge you'd be a corpse before you even knew something was wrong."

"Then how the hell do the Nárva survive here?"

"By some scientific definitions," Rogan replied matter-of-factly, "they don't."

More ships fled past them. Streams of spacecraft flowed across the ruinous landscape, converging where the great peaks and troughs of what Adi had called the Valleys of Cykyrus met before rocketing up towards the cosmos. In the distance, ahead and to either side of the ship, lay the glittering lights of towering Nárva cities. Judging by the *Adeona's* trajectory, Jack guessed Grand Minister Zsal could be found inside the one at the far end of the aforementioned gorge.

Jack flinched as something swept past the side of their ship, instantly assuming it was the Prymalis or a Nárva gunship mistaking them for a threat. Whatever it was had followed them from one of the barren mountain peaks rising like crones' fingers from the sterile earth. But their unexpected neighbour appeared as nothing but a fleeting shadow, a brief puff of black smoke belched from a factory chimney. To Jack's horror, he suddenly realised it was some form of winged beast billowing back and forth on the toxic wind.

"That," he said, pointing numbly out the window, "is a bloody wraith."

"It's not a ghost," Rogan said kindly. "I've studied your species' history, Jack. Wraiths, ghosts, ghouls – they aren't real. What you're seeing outside is the Vekemorte equivalent of a raven, or an eagle."

"That's nothing like an eagle, Rogan! It looks... it looks undead!"

"I told you to brace yourself, didn't I?"

The wraith (no matter what Rogan said, Jack couldn't see it as anything else) banked right, away from the ship. Leathery ribbons trailed out behind its emaciated, ephemeral wings like ghostly tendrils. From a black, bony skull, admittedly sporting an unmistakable beak, gazed dark, eyeless sockets. Two additional members of its family swept over the *Adeona* to join it, and they descended towards the valleys together.

"Every square inch of the planet's atmosphere is infected by spores released by the Ch'greth fungus," Rogan said, finally deciding she owed Jack an explanation. "Nothing with skin or delicate tissue can survive. Bone is fine – even those as brittle as yours, Jack – as are the hardier and rather unique organs developed by creatures on Veke-morte. Any species capable of regeneration might last for a little while, though it certainly wouldn't wish to. The emergence of sophisticated organisms should have been impossible here. But life did evolve nonetheless, and in such a manner to best fit its environment, hence the fauna's rather... *macabre* appearance."

"It's why the Grand Minister wears such a complicated and restrictive suit everywhere she goes," Tuner added. "In the same way any other organic can't step foot on her planet without instantly dying, she's extremely vulnerable everywhere else."

Jack shuddered at the thought of Zsal's appearance underneath that complicated array of metal gauntlets and uncomfortable breathing apparatus. Hey, what was the point of imagining? He'd probably discover what she looked like soon enough.

"And the two of you aren't affected?" he asked the automata. "What about the *Adeona's* hull?"

"Not even at risk of tarnishing," Tuner replied proudly. "The spores only attack organic matter, thankfully."

"Oh, yes." Jack pursed his lips and nodded. "Very thankfully. Hold on. If nothing on Vekemorte has evolved to feature tissue or, you know, normal organs and other fleshy stuff... what the hell does anything on this planet *eat?*"

"The fungus," Rogan replied. "Everything's already immune to it, after all. And it's spread everywhere, due to its rather aggressive form of pollination. What scientists believe to have originally been a survival tactic to avoid being eaten has certainly not played out in the mushroom's favour."

"So despite everything in this world looking like it's out of a cheese-induced nightmare, all of its animals are vegetarian. That's reassuring, I suppose."

"Fungivores, technically," Rogan said. "But yes. Nothing is going to try and eat you."

"But don't assume the local fauna won't kill you just for the fun of it," Tuner said brightly. "Some can be quite territorial."

"Here's some more of that fauna now," Adi said as they dropped even closer to ground level. "A herd just outside the window, port side. Friendly, I hope."

Adi enlarged the view slightly so the crew could observe better from a safe distance. Jack crossed the cockpit and gave the scene outside a tentative glance. About a dozen tusked creatures, built like buffalo or oxen, stampeded across the murky plains, most likely startled by all the explosive commotion in the upper atmosphere. A couple of the herd's number were smaller than the rest – calves, most likely. The idea that such beings could breed was still beyond Jack's comprehension, however. As far as he was concerned, these weren't living creatures – they were skeletons held together by scraps of ossified tendons and, well, dark-bloody-magic. He could see their stone-like organs swinging about inside their rib cages, for heaven's sake!

"All this time spent exploring the galaxy," Rogan said, placing a caring hand on Jack's shoulder, "and you still don't get it. There's more to this universe than any mere mortal could ever hope to understand."

"Sure, but what about you?" he asked slyly.

"I can't explain it any better than you can," she replied. "Well, not *much* better, perhaps. But I do know that harsh challenges breed strong survivors. And I'm built from gears and pistons and cables, none of which you find in what constitutes 'normal' nature. If I can function, why shouldn't they?"

"Erm, guys?" Tuner jumped onto the dashboard and jabbed a tiny finger at the window. "I think I might have found what those beasties were running from!"

Two black specks were fast approaching on the ship's starboard side. This time, however, there was no hope they were weird spectral birds indigenous to the planet. Their spiky, trilobite-shaped hulls were much scarier.

"Prymalis attack ships," Rogan said, racing back to the hologram table. "Bolts. Adi, get us out of here, now!"

"At their present velocity, I'll never be able to escape Vekemorte's atmosphere before they catch us," the *Adeona* replied.

"We can lose them in the Valleys of Cykyrus," Jack said, jabbing a thumb over his shoulder at the intricate network of dark gulches below. "You know the drill, Adi. I'll navigate the tight corners, you operate the guns."

"With pleasure," the ship replied, handing Jack the controls.

He immediately sent the *Adeona* into a steep dive. Gone

was the vista of misshapen mountains and fortified cities, replaced instantly by a cavernous crack that lacerated the desiccated world. Jack didn't know how far or how deep it went, only that the Valleys held the secret to their survival.

He hoped.

"How's it looking behind us?" Jack shouted as they shot into darkness. Adi applied a night-vision filter to the windows; they didn't dare switch on the floodlights in case they gave their position away.

"Both Prymalis ships are still heading straight for our position," Rogan replied. Adi's scans floated above the hologram table. "They'll be inside the canyon within the next six seconds."

"Maybe they'll fly right over," Tuner said. "We don't know for sure they even saw us."

"Maybe," Jack replied, shoving the accelerator lever forwards. "But do you honestly want to take that risk?"

He took a deep breath and concentrated on the route ahead. He had his job, Adi had hers. At least he'd thought to put on his space suit before they set off. Now the atmosphere wouldn't kill him the instant the *Adeona* suffered a hull breach.

The sides of the canyon tapered towards one another as they descended into the bowels of the earth, and Jack was reluctant to bring the ship too low in case it impeded his ability to manoeuvre. Smaller cracks and valleys and gulches split off in all directions, but he kept the *Adeona* racing straight forward in order to maintain her escalating pace.

"They just banked hard into the canyon," Rogan said. "They're definitely following us."

"Thought so. We need a destination, Adi. Somewhere to head towards in case we can't lose them in here."

"Grand Minister Zsal is presently inside the walls of Neceyro," the ship replied. "That's the city directly ahead. Technically, we could follow the Valleys right to it, provided we follow the correct route."

"We can't lead the Prymalis attack ship towards innocent people!" Tuner exclaimed.

"We won't," Jack yelled back. "But given our track record of fighting these things, we might need to lead them towards somebody with a bit more firepower. I'm sure the Nárva have ships defending their city."

"Not that we won't try to get rid of them first," the *Adeona* added mischievously, warming up her cannons.

"Your NavMap route is online," Rogan said as green arrows splashed over the cockpit windows in front of Jack. "Little chance of it changing on the fly this time, fortunately."

Jack growled in his throat as he recalled the debacle of piloting through Yanna Lös's collapsing ice tunnels.

"And for once I can fly right out of here if things get too hairy," he muttered to himself.

"They're closing in," Rogan said urgently.

Jack turned sharp left into the next fissure. He didn't doubt the Prymalis saw where they went. The immediate right into a narrow crack that ran parallel to the main canyon was much more likely to throw them off, and it barely required them to go off-route.

"They're still following," Rogan said.

"Brilliant," Jack grunted.

Though the Valleys of Cykyrus were natural in origin, many of the walls sported signs of Nárva culture, namely ancient pillars that were cracked and collapsing but also more than a few statues taller than the Great Sphinx of Giza. Some depicted monstrous beasts native to Vekemorte or Nárva mythology (apparently, it was hard to tell the difference), others the Nárva themselves, presumably – Jack could only clock them as blurs in his peripheral vision as they whizzed past.

He banked left, ascending clumsily to avoid the elevated canyon floor. They were back following the NavMap route. The Prymalis attack ships continued catching up to them.

"Are they within range of your cannons, Adi?"

"Not yet," the *Adeona* replied. "We can be sure they'll let us know when they are…"

"What about using your guns to bring part of the Valley down on them? Or to block their path, or something?"

"You want to destroy the Valleys of Cykyrus?" Rogan shook her head. "It's a sacred and protected natural landmark older than anything in mankind's history. You think the Prymalis are bad? The Nárva would skin you alive just for scribbling on it in crayon."

"Okay." Jack shrugged. "Maybe we won't deface a priceless Nárva World Heritage site right before asking their ambassador for a favour. It was just a thought."

A projectile shot past the window and blew the head off an ancient stone monster.

"Shame the Prymalis don't have quite the same reverence for history we do," he shouted, swerving hard to the other side of the valley. "Can you start shooting yet, Adi?"

"With pleasure," she replied.

The two Prymalis attack ships followed the *Adeona* down the valley – for the time being, there was nowhere else for them to go but up. With one rotary cannon she filled the centre of the valley with ballistic rounds; with the other, she drew rings around the duo – the same tactic she used with some degree of success back inside the porous floating mountains of XO-R15.

One Prymalis ship hit its air brakes hard and quickly rose out of the trench. The other followed Adi's ring of death in a manner Jack could almost describe as mocking. The former lost one of its many craggy spines during its rapid ascent but suffered no further damage.

"Either the Prymalis operate as a hive-mind," the *Adeona* said, embarrassed, "or their pilots have been warned about us. I can't seem to land a decent hit."

"I suppose that explains why these ships are so eager to hunt us down," Jack said through gritted teeth. "Keep trying, Adi. In the meantime, I'll keep looking for somewhere that might catch them off guard..."

"Could you use Adi's air brakes to stop suddenly, let them shoot past us, and then blow them up from behind?" Tuner asked, hurrying down the cockpit to stand beside him. "I think I saw a pilot do it in a human film once."

Jack barked out a slightly unhinged laugh as another projectile skimmed their shields.

"If I was flying a fighter jet, maybe. But the *Adeona*, inside an atmosphere as thick as this? Adi's tough, but she's not built for combat manoeuvres. The sudden change in acceleration might tear her hull in half."

"Let's try to avoid that," Adi said, continuing to fire streams of ballistic rounds at the approaching Prymalis ships. "I've only just gotten over my last accident."

"Head down," Rogan said calmly.

"What?" Jack shouted over his shoulder.

"Head *down!*"

The valley suddenly ended where an enormous dip in the world began. Circular, bowl-shaped, busy with malformed geological anomalies, and savagely overgrown with luminous green fungi. Jack sent the *Adeona* into a dive and then stuck close to the ground as it levelled out again, her thrusters kicking up a thick cloud of dust in their wake.

"Let me guess," Jack said, flexing his trembling fingers around the flight stick. "The *Crater* of Cykyrus?"

"Got it in one," Rogan replied.

"Also known as a wide open space with nowhere to hide," Tuner added, anxiously inspecting Adi's readouts.

"Unfortunately," Jack said, punching the accelerator lever forwards again, "I think we're long past the point of hiding."

He swerved the *Adeona* back and forth between the rock formations. Tuner was right – there was nowhere to settle the ship down and wait for the Prymalis to grow bored. And they had to assume such a technologically advanced species possessed some form of radar or scanning system. Trying to hide behind one of the crater's bulky geological features would only get them killed even quicker.

"They're still following," Rogan said. "In fact, they're matching your bearing move for move."

"I'm never gonna lose them. Adi, any luck with those guns? Surely the Nárva don't care as much about *these* rocks."

"Unfortunately, your erratic piloting means that I rarely get more than a microsecond to take aim before I lose sight of them again," the ship replied. "Not that I'm complaining, mind you. If I can't shoot them, they can't shoot us."

"Unless they have homing missiles," Tuner said.

"Very helpful," Rogan said to him sternly.

Jack swung the *Adeona* under a narrow rock-bridge; the two Prymalis ships followed with ease. Squeezing between a pair of decrepit pillars proved no greater a challenge.

"Hold on," said Rogan, studying her scans of the immediate area. "Something in this crater moved."

"Bloody hell." Jack shook his head. "This planet's freaky enough without the damn rocks wandering about."

"Bolts alive, I'm not sure they are... Bank right over that boulder."

"Sure, why not." Jack did as asked.

"And now curve around, sticking close to the big white monolith," Rogan added. "Avoiding the jagged cave full of stalactites, if you can."

"You know, we're deviating quite a lot from the advised NavMap route..." Jack's eyes grew wide and his mouth dry. "Oh. I see. Well, that's quite alarming."

"And now, if you would," Rogan said as calmly as possible, "please get us out of here as fast as you can."

"My pleasure," he said, pushing the lever forwards. "Extra juice please, Adi!"

"Giving myself everything I've got, Captain!"

They swung back into a passage just as the Prymalis attack ships burst into the clearing behind them, perfectly following the curvature of Jack's own trajectory. A pair of explosive projectiles detonated against the rocks to either side of the *Adeona*. She shook violently enough for her shields to flicker.

"I fear they won't miss next time," Adi warned Jack.

"With any luck," Rogan said, "they won't get another chance."

Both Prymalis attack ships continued their chase. One of them almost scraped its rear spines against the big white monolith occupying the bulk of the clearing. Had they flown using conventional thrusters, they surely would have scorched a long, black mark against the pearly rock.

They straightened out, ready to follow.

And, slowly, the big white monolith stood up behind them.

"Not a rock," Jack mumbled to himself in disbelief.

The gigantic creature rose to full height – it must have measured seventy metres or more – and roared with a head like that of a fleshless snapper turtle. The series of boulders to either side rearranged themselves into arms and legs. It seemed as if this colossus had evolved not to sport an exoskeleton exactly, but instead to simply grow all of its regular bones on the outside. Wisps of the same ephemeral darkness Jack had seen on the flying wraiths billowed out from its otherwise hollow rib cage.

With a swing of its giant, prehistorical claw, it grabbed one of the Prymalis ships before it could accelerate away, pulled the struggling vessel up to its skull, and bit down hard. The other decided enough was enough and shot up out of the Valleys.

"You know," Jack said, "I really don't think I like this planet."

He winced as the colossus continued to chow down on the ancient ship. Not a pleasant way to go. But presuming the Prymalis were as susceptible to the Ch'greth fungus as every other species in the galaxy, the poor bastard wouldn't suffer for long.

"Crevice," Rogan said. "Far side."

Jack weaved the *Adeona* through the eerie rock formations as gracefully as his shaking hands allowed, hoping there weren't any more monstrous skeletons hiding among their number. For a planet so inhospitable, it sure liked turning un-living things alive.

He guided the ship through the crevice and the NavMap arrows flickered back onto his windscreen. The skyscrapers of Neceyro stood proudly beyond the high walls of the canyon. From a glance, it looked as if it was a straight shot through this one last Valley before they reached the city gates.

"Almost there, guys," Jack said with a relieved sigh. "Christ alive. That was a close one."

"I thought they had us," Tuner said, emerging from underneath one of the computer terminals. "If it hadn't been for that *ossis mortuus*..."

"No use in worrying about that now." Jack exhaled deeply, controlled his breathing. "We're in the—"

The ship lurched forwards with a deep *boom*. Jack struggled to keep her steady. The shields, normally invisible, sparked a bright electric blue, died, and then crackled into life again.

"The remaining Prymalis ship is back," Adi announced. "I've taken a direct hit to one of my rear thrusters, though my shields absorbed ninety percent of the impact. Damage is minimal, but we won't survive another strike."

"Goddammit." Jack scoured the valley for a way out. "And there's nowhere else for us to go."

"Incoming missile!"

Jack banked left; the missile soared past only a few feet from the cockpit window. He quickly swerved far over to the right to avoid the attack ship's follow-up attack.

"We won't survive long in this trench," Rogan shouted over the wail of the *Adeona's* alarms. "Do something, Jack!"

"You're the genius, Rogan! Do *what?*"

"Erm, guys?" Tuner retreated back to his hiding spot. "Looks like the Prymalis aren't our only problem!"

Jack squinted far ahead to the end of the final valley. What he saw made his eyes open up wide again.

"Oh, bloody hell..."

A grand wall of Vekemortean stone and metal ringed Neceyro. From the two towers of an antiquated gatehouse that once opened out onto the Valleys of Cykyrus rose a pair of industrial rail guns the length of Boeing Triple-7s. Jack had seen cannons like that eliminate whole battlecruisers with a single shot, but never one attached to anything other than another ship or space station.

"Those rail guns are ridiculous!" Rogan screamed in exasperation. "What do the Nárva think they're doing, deploying weapons like that?"

"Wouldn't you, if you had giant undead monsters on your doorstep?"

"Yes, Jack, but why do they have them pointed at *us?*"

Jack went to conjure a snappy retort, then bit his tongue. It was a good question, actually. The rail guns had certainly swivelled to face their direction, but the *Adeona* wasn't the only ship heading towards the city...

"I'm not certain they are. Hold on!"

He yanked the flight stick back and sent the *Adeona* on a breakneck climb towards the heavens. Naturally, the Prymalis ship followed suit a split-second later. Jack gritted his teeth, gripped the controls so hard his hands fell into cramps, and tried not to shut his eyes.

One of the rail guns fired. There was no explosion of noise. The only evidence that the weapon had even been fired was the piercing crackle of electricity as its magnets launched a projectile at speeds close to Mach Eight.

The sound wave rocked the *Adeona* milliseconds later. Jack relaxed, but only slightly. His hunch must have been correct. They weren't the chosen target.

"How's it looking behind us, Adi?"

"It's looking pretty nice, Jack." The ship sounded even more elated than he felt. "That Prymalis ship is falling back into the canyon in approximately six thousand different pieces. It's going to be one heck of a clean-up job."

"Yes, wonderful," Rogan said impatiently. "But just because the Nárva blew up one ship doesn't mean they won't try to shoot us down, too."

Jack nervously brought the *Adeona* level with the city of Neceyro once more. The rail guns tracked them diligently. They'd have little warning if one of them fired, and there'd be no getting out of their way.

Tuner slowly elevated his head so that it poked over the lip of the cockpit dashboard.

"Do you think we should back away slowly?" he whispered.

Everybody jumped as a scratchy voice burst through the comms system. Well, Jack did. The two automata at least had the grace to act surprised.

"Crew of the *Adeona*, this is Neceyro Ground Control. Do you read?"

"Yes, Ground Control," Rogan quickly replied. "We read you loud and clear. Thank you for the assist back there. It was greatly appreciated."

"You've been cleared to enter the city airspace," the operator continued after a momentary pause. "I suggest you land post-haste, before you bring any more unwanted attention our way."

The comm channel closed abruptly. Jack whistled as he handed full control back to the ship.

"I don't know why I expected a warm reception," he said, leaning back in his chair. "If I lived in this hellscape, I wouldn't feel very hospitable either."

4

NÁRVA IN NECEYRO

Jack triple-checked his suit before the *Adeona* sacrificed the integrity of her artificial atmosphere to the hostile air outside. Then he asked Tuner to give it the thrice-over, just in case.

"I wouldn't worry too much," the little automata said, peering at the seals between his torso and leg pieces. "If there is a hole, you won't even know it."

"If it's so quick," Jack asked suspiciously, "how does anyone know it isn't painful? The process of death might only last a second, but maybe to the person who inhales the spores it feels like drowning in a vat of acid for eternity."

"Oh, I'm sure they've done experiments on prisoners and the like," Tuner cheerfully replied. "During darker years, of course. The Nárva would never be so uncivilised now."

"Unless somebody had just led a destructive chase through their sacred Valleys of Cykyrus, perhaps."

"Hmm. Yes, perhaps. Your suit is fine, Jack."

"Absolutely sure?"

"Please don't ask me to check it again…"

"Come on, you two," said Rogan, standing beside the button that lowered the *Adeona's* loading ramp. "There's a galactic war going on right above our heads. The longer we dally about here, the greater the chance Neceyro gets glassed."

"Oh, that *really* makes me excited to leave the ship." Jack nodded at the button; Rogan pressed it.

Jack could see the spores as soon as the ramp descended. The air was thick with it, as if he were walking through the mist of a sauna. It tinted everything a sickly green colour. He could still see a fair distance outside of the ship – a hundred metres, maybe less – but any further than that and all the details became foggy. He flinched back as it enveloped first Rogan and Tuner, and then his spacesuit.

Well, he wasn't dead yet. He guessed that meant his suit was airtight, and scribbled down a mental note not to make any unnecessary lunges. On Vekemorte, a bullet grazing his armour could be even deadlier than a direct hit.

A flash of panic, then relief as Jack remembered they'd sealed the pantry door shut. Most of his supplies came in tins, but if any spores got into the food they'd have to space the whole lot to be safe.

God, he hated this planet already.

He reluctantly followed the two automata down the ramp.

If he had to be brutally honest, and given his experience of the planet so far he felt as if he'd earned the right, Neceyro wasn't particularly aesthetically pleasing. Maybe it was just the fungus, which seemed to not only permeate the air with its spores but also grow sporadically over the buildings and even more so along the gutters of the streets. The Nárva ate the fungi, Jack understood, as did every other form of life on Vekemorte. So what separated the fungi they had for breakfast, lunch and dinner from those that sprouted between the cracks in the pavement? He supposed that having a source of nutrition so abundant that it could be found on every street corner was one way to combat poverty.

Jack realised his breathing was heavy and tried to calm it. He wasn't at risk of running out of oxygen. He just really didn't want another debilitating panic attack in the middle of a toxic city under siege by an alien superpower. This was something approximating a diplomatic mission – they went in, they had a chat, and they got out. Nothing else to worry about.

It wasn't just the spores or the overenthusiastic fungi, Jack decided. The city was just plain ugly. Had they landed in a deprived part of town, he wondered? A few of the corporate skyscrapers were constructed in interestingly coiled, hexagonal and even abstractly netted exoskeletal designs – similar, in fact, to the bone-ribbed battlecruisers currently in orbit around their planet – but the vast majority of buildings were blocky and drab. Not primitive, but any means. It went without saying that even the most basic Neceyro home possessed technological innovations far beyond anything of which humanity could boast. But characterless, as if the Nárva had zero taste for anything except pure, untainted functionality.

The revelation was sudden and sharp enough to stop Jack in his tracks.

"Rogan... are the Nárva blind?"

She looked at him as if he'd asked whether water was wet or if Krolaks liked their teeth cleaned.

"Why of course they are," she replied. "Every species on Vekemorte is. I highly doubt any creature in the galaxy has evolved an eyeball that won't dissolve in this atmosphere."

She tapped one of her eye lenses. "Nothing organic, at any rate. The Nárva use sound to experience their environment in a process similar to echolocation. It's extremely accurate, so don't assume you could get the upper hand on one in a fight. They can see even better than you in terms of navigating their physical environment. They simply use a different set of waves, which unfortunately, from your perspective, excludes the spectrum of colour. It's quite common, really. It was only a few days ago you first encountered the Kwoo Fim, remember?"

"Well, that certainly explains the lack of exterior design," Jack mumbled. "I'm not sure it makes them any less creepy."

"You think not having eyes makes them creepy?" Rogan scoffed. "Careful, Jack. You've got squishy balls of goo in your head that catch and convert wavelengths of light so you can see rainbows. What must they think of you?"

"Yeah, good point. Thanks for reminding me I'm just a big, walking sack of delicate meat."

"You consider yourself a delicacy?" Tuner asked.

"I said delicate, Tuner."

"Oh."

"Did you not read anything in the dossier I sent you?" Rogan asked irritably.

"I skimmed it." Jack shrugged. "There was rather a lot. Are the streets usually this empty?"

"Of course not. Neceyro is a powerful, thriving Nárva hub. I imagine most of its citizens have either evacuated or retreated to underground bunkers, however. Given the choice, I wouldn't be wandering around outside either."

"So why are we?" Jack glanced each way down the deserted alleys. It was like walking through a post-nuclear wasteland. "Do we actually have any idea where we're going?"

"I'm not an idiot, Jack." Rogan rolled her eye-lenses. "We didn't come all the way to a world battling the Prymalis just to go knocking door to door. Adi got to work triangulating the Grand Minister's position as soon as we entered Vekemorte's airspace. She's almost certainly holed up in the Brahgii Centre."

"I presume she knows we're coming," Tuner added. "I'd be surprised if Ground Control would have let us into the city otherwise, what with us being chased by the enemy and all."

"And where's this Brahgii Centre?" Jack asked.

"Four minutes from here. Three if you concentrate on walking instead of staring at everything we pass with those goo balls of yours."

Jack quit asking questions, but his eyes couldn't help wandering. It was incredible how much the spores masked the sky – staring at the heavens should have revealed a couple of Prymalis warships, if not more. They were closest to Vekemorte's atmosphere, after all, no doubt hoping to use their solar beams to cripple the planet in the same way they had Paryx. That they hadn't already was testament to the strength of the Nárva armada. But all he saw was a murky cloud of green and the occasional flash like lightning as nuclear torpedoes detonated out in the heliosphere.

The Brahgii Centre was a huge pyramid surrounded by resplendent fountains. Jack was surprised to see water flowing in such a horrid environment, but it made sense. Few creatures in the galaxy could survive without it, and even those required some kind of regular substitute in their diet. If the Nárva could eat the Ch'greth fungus, there was no reason they couldn't safely drink the water it infected, too. As for the Centre itself, there was something about its facade that gave him a disconcerting sense of deja vu.

It clicked. Of course. The exterior of the Ministerium for Cultured Planets, he realised. The Nárva were one of the most influential species in the galaxy – of course they'd have a hand in designing the council's headquarters, too.

A good few dozen guards stood outside of its doors, along with hover-tanks and anti-aircraft cannons – miniature versions of those protecting the city walls. Each humanoid guard was kitted out in anonymous black, glossy body armour from head to toe and appeared utterly unbothered by the tiny, furry spores settling over them like green snowflakes. They moved as one to block the crew's path as soon as they climbed the Centre's steps.

"Can't let you in," one of the guards said, their voice muffled by the helmet. "Turn around and seek shelter."

"You don't understand," Jack said, pushing past Rogan. "We're here to speak to Grand Minister Zsal. It's about—"

"We don't care what it's about," another guard snapped. "We have executive orders not to let anyone into the building, not even citizens. It's not safe here. Vacate the premises or we will be forced to incarcerate you."

"Will that get us inside the building?" Tuner asked. "Because if so..."

The first guard put a hand on the second's helmet, an apparently friendly gesture.

"Let them through," they said. "Just got word from up top. They're cleared for entry."

The second guard studied the crew carefully and gripped its plasma rifle tight. Jack started to suspect they'd be turned away, or worse. Then suddenly it beckoned for them to follow.

"Right. You three, come with me. Do everything I say, or

I'll shoot you. Shouldn't be letting outsiders in here at a time like this."

Another pair of guards opened the doors for them and everyone filed through. The interior of the Bahgii Centre looked nothing like that of the Ministry, which made sense given the latter's similarity to the main base of the Prymalis, who were the architects of both. Where there was any colour, it appeared in splotchy and inconsistent patterns that clashed with everything else. A central elevator strut ran through the core of the pyramid and its various floors; from its base, Jack stared up through ring upon ring of glass right up to its pointed tip, which allowed natural green light to permeate every level. The guard pressed a keycard to a reader embedded in the strut's wall and a concealed (though Jack suspected not remotely secret to any visiting Nárva) door slid aside. Inside was an elevator into which Jack, Rogan and Tuner were promptly hurried.

The elevator shot downwards. Jack supposed it was sensible to keep everybody who still remained inside the building on as low a floor as possible, given the likelihood of attack. He couldn't tell how deep the elevator went, but the doors hissed open again only a few seconds later.

Still no decorations; still no form that didn't entirely serve function. There weren't even any statues lining the walls, which Jack knew the Nárva could appreciate the same way the squishy Kwoo Fim creatures they rescued from Yanna Lös evidently did. As they were marched down a pitch-black corridor Jack wondered if he still held certain presumptions and prejudices, despite the insane degree of diversity he'd witnessed throughout the galaxy. The idea that a whole species could lack a sense he took completely for granted and be no worse the wear for it continued to baffle him, yet he knew there were empires whose perceptual abilities made Jack seem as if he were permanently stuck inside a sensory deprivation tank.

Still just a stupid human, he supposed. If it weren't for the night vision filter inside his helmet, he'd be smacking his head into the walls.

Another door hissed open. They were ushered in, the door locked shut again, and then the guard stood to attention to one side. The room was full with Nárva working at undulating pods. A giant display hovered above a war table, but it wasn't a hologram, which for obvious reasons would have been of little use to the operatives. It was a floating orb of solid matter that shape-shifted into diagrams and maps and patterns of brail which the surrounding ring of Nárva could quickly study with a wave of their hand.

A figure in a long, black robe at the front of the war table turned to greet them.

Jack tried not to gasp. He was certain everyone in the room would hear it.

Grand Minister Zsal – if it hadn't been for the Ministry robe, he wouldn't have known it was her – had scarcely any face to speak of. Her small, white skull was misshapen and cratered like the moons of Jupiter, and she possessed neither eyes or eye sockets, nor any nose or ears that Jack could see. The only aspect which Jack found familiar was her wide, lipless mouth full of flat molars. No incisors, thank God. Her four metal gauntlets were gone in addition to her breathing apparatus, and her exposed hands looked as if they'd only recently been robbed from a grave.

Compared to the Nárva, a Therek like Gaskan Troi was the sort of friendly face suitable for children's birthday parties.

"Mr. Bishop," she said in a raspy voice like sand slipping through an hourglass. "Rogan. And Tuner, wasn't it? Can you see all right? I've recently been made aware that our Command Centre isn't exactly accommodating for foreign guests."

"We all have night vision," Rogan replied kindly. "We can see you just fine, Grand Minister."

"Good. Now you can explain what you think you're doing, flying into restricted airspace during an active military operation. Which part of 'I don't have time for this' didn't you three understand?"

Rogan and Tuner glanced at Jack. He sighed. Great. It *had* been his plan to come here, so it was only fair he be the one to face the ambassador's ire.

"In fairness, we didn't properly receive your message," Jack said, swallowing hard. "You were cutting in and out due to the, erm, radioactive disturbances in your upper atmosphere."

"Most intelligent beings would take that as a sign to stay away," Zsal replied, folding her skeletal hands over one another. "So what should that tell me about you?"

"That what we have to say is really important," Rogan said, crossing her arms. "Maybe even more important than the fight for this world, in fact."

The Grand Minister tilted her head as if listening, though nobody save for the other Nárva made any noise. Jack guessed she was studying their body language.

"Explain," she finally said.

"We have reason to believe that the Prymalis are converging towards a key location," Jack said. "Their attacks might appear random, and I guess to an extent they are, but ultimately all of their ships are headed towards one planet in particular. Kapamentis."

"Kapamentis?" Zsal's skull tilted the other way. "You're sure of this? It hardly poses a military threat."

"I've run extrapolative simulations," Rogan replied. "We can be about eighty-three percent certain that's where the Prymalis are going. It might be all of them, it might be a single ship. There's no way of knowing. But they're sending *something* there, and they're going to great lengths to cover their intentions. No other scenario has even remotely similar odds of probability."

"Kapamentis. By the gods." Zsal shook her head, brushed the floating orb with one of her four hands. "One of the most populated worlds in the whole Ministerium and only a few hand-me-down Ministry frigates to defend it. It'll be a massacre."

"Exactly! Now you can see why it was so important we come and speak to you!"

The Grand Minister continued to study the symbols on the orb that flittered gracefully past her hand. Whatever she read caused her to bow her head.

"The battle above Vekemorte continues to rage without the tide ebbing one way or the other," she announced. "Every time we disable one of the enemy warships, another of our own battlecruisers takes a fatal hit. We'll win this fight, I think. We have to. But we won't be prepared for a second attack until reinforcements arrive, and sending more ships here puts one of our other colonies at risk. Do you understand me?"

Jack opened and closed his mouth in disbelief.

"You're saying you won't help, aren't you?"

"No, Mr. Jack Bishop." Zsal snapped her hand away from the display. "I'm saying that *nobody* will help, not when their own homeworld is under threat of invasion or destruction. It's not a matter of personal opinion – if I could justify sending ships to defend Kapamentis, I would. That planet has become more of a home to me than Vekemorte, believe me. But even if an attack were guaranteed – which, despite your assertions, it is not – sending a fleet to Kapamentis would simply be out of the question for the exact same reason we haven't assigned any to help our less fortunate neighbours. The potential loss of Nárva lives is not a cost we are prepared to pay."

"You think that by helping another," Rogan asked incredulously, "you in turn sacrifice yourself?"

"In this case, yes. Unfortunate, I understand. Cold, even. But the Nárva must protect themselves before they rush to anyone else's aid. Otherwise they can succeed at neither."

"Even a single Nárva battlecruiser could help defend one of the smaller species' worlds and save millions of lives," Jack said through gritted teeth. "Fine. We can't convince you, or you can't convince your own superiors, or whatever. I get it. But Ministry council or no Ministry council, you still hold a lot of sway in this galaxy, Zsal. Put a call out to every member species, past and present. Tell them what's going to happen. You can't spare any ships, sure, but they might."

"From my decades spent liaising with... shall we say *difficult* individuals, I can assure you that they won't. The Ministerium didn't disband because the galactic community wished to stand together in unison, Jack. We're a selfish bunch, especially those who've the most to lose. Besides, it's a moot point. Even if I was inclined to embarrass myself, I don't have the means. Sending out such a call would require returning to the Ministerium headquarters, and I refuse to abandon Vekemorte during a crisis such as this."

"Why would you need to go to Kapamentis?" Tuner asked. "I thought Jack and Klik made an emergency broadcast from Minister Keeto's ship once. Why can't you just send something from here?"

"Minister Keeto's comm unit may have been dialled into an internal Ministry frequency," Zsal explained, "but her ship certainly wouldn't have had the range, let alone access to the Mass Address Channel. You're talking about sending a direct message to the leaders of more than a hundred thousand empires. Only a Grand Minister is permitted to do that, for obvious reasons, and even then only from the Ministerium chamber itself."

Tuner threw his hands in the air.

"But there's nobody there anymore! You were the last to leave!"

Zsal, who appeared more concerned with caressing the warping brown globe than their present conversation, paused.

"Yes," she said. "I was. And as the person tasked with shutting everything down, I also retain access should the Ministerium ever require reinstatement. Perhaps my authority could return to Kapamentis even if my physical presence remains here."

Zsal quickly crossed the room to stand inches from Jack, who tried his best not to flinch at the sight of her ghastly, featureless face.

"Take my data pad," she said quietly, handing it to him. "It's wiped save for my access details, so don't think you'll find any member state's secrets in there. It'll give you clearance for both the chamber and the official comm channel. Send out your own plea for assistance if you truly think any will come."

"Thank you," Rogan said. "You may have just saved Kapamentis."

"I wish I shared your optimism. I'm not yet convinced I can save my own homeworld. Now, the three of you had best go. You've taken up enough of my time – gods, you shouldn't have come to Vekemorte in the first place. Officer, please escort Jack and his companions back to their ship."

"You can't focus only on your own people," Jack said as he was marched brusquely from the Command Centre. "Sooner or later, every empire in the galaxy needs to put aside their differences and take a stand."

"I don't disagree with you," Zsal called after him distractedly. "The problem we face, Mr. Bishop, is that every empire wishes to stand alone."

5

CRUD AND DESPAIR

J ack had been busy scrolling through encyclopaedic entries on as many species as he could find to expand his understanding of galactic biodiversity when the *Adeona* suddenly lurched out of subspace. It was an abrupt and clumsy stop quite at odds with the ship's usual grace, and they were still fifteen minutes out from their destination. Fifteen minutes over the course of thousands of light years was within a reasonable margin as far as Jack was concerned, but given that Rogan was running the calculations instead of him, it quite possibly amounted to a catastrophic error.

He quickly checked out the window of his quarters. Yep, they were definitely back in regular space. And much to his relief, nothing appeared to have exploded.

"What happened, Adi?" he said, bursting out of his room and hurrying up to the cockpit. "Are we at Kapamentis already? Or did we hit something?"

"Neither," Rogan replied, casually pointing at the windows as he rushed past. "We've just run into some unexpected traffic."

Hundreds of ramshackle ships streamed past the front of the *Adeona* in a long train stretching as far as Jack's eyes could see. Most vessels were small, family-sized, with more room allocated for storage than their passengers. Sprinkled amongst their number were larger colony ships – giant, coiled bowling balls carried by great solar sails. The hull of every spacecraft was painted with the same cursive, red iconography.

"What is it?" Jack asked. "Some kind of refugee convoy?"

"It appears to be a Sh'ddeh Burrai caravan," Rogan replied. "A whole community taking the slow route to Sobbo Tau, by the look of it. It would be quicker to travel individually, but safer as a group. I can't say they'll be much better off on Sobbo Tau than Kapamentis, though. At least not for long."

"Do you think somebody else has figured out the Prymalis' pattern?" Tuner asked, his LED eyes brightening with hope. "Is that why people are leaving?"

"Maybe, but I wouldn't bet on it." Rogan shook her head. "I imagine they're headed someplace quieter because they see which way the wind is blowing, to borrow a human phrase. With so many planets getting attacked, it's almost inevitable that Kapamentis will be targeted sooner or later."

"Well," Jack added, "if it adds a few days or weeks to their lives, who can blame them? They're in no better state to fight the Prymalis than we are."

The train continued to file past with no sign of trickling to a stop. Tired of drifting awkwardly (and of being stared at by the alien faces peering out the convoy's various windows), the *Adeona* took a slow, wide dive around their unexpected obstacle. Even once clear on the other side, the glittery black orb of Kapamentis was nowhere in sight.

"Only a short skip to our destination," the ship

announced to her crew. "If you've anything to prepare before you disembark, you'd better do it now."

FOR THE FIRST time in the history of the galaxy, it was easy to find a parking spot on Kapamentis.

They had money to pay the fee – the financial reserves of Detri were deep, given that few if any of its citizens had any need for credits – but nobody to whom they could pay it. Adi sought the same port she used the first time she came to Kapamentis with Jack and her automata crew, knowing it to be within walking distance of the Ministry headquarters yet far enough away not to invoke an eye-watering bill. But less than a quarter of the hundred-odd bays were occupied when they arrived, and noticeably fewer ships came than went. The scrap-metal pedestrian doors at the front of the stadium-port were thrown as wide open as the ginormous retractable ceiling, and no wardens patrolled the dirt. The proprietor must have been even quicker to jump planet than his customers.

Jack descended the *Adeona's* loading ramp and took a deep breath of sludgy, neon-singed air. It wasn't fresher than that which his spacesuit produced, and it certainly wasn't healthier for him, but there was still something reassuringly real about inhaling a planet's atmosphere – terraformed or not. Plus, not wearing a helmet meant he didn't have to constantly pretend that his nose wasn't itching.

"It's a bit different from the first time you were here, isn't it?" said Tuner, waddling to a stop beside him.

"Yeah," Jack mumbled. "You could say that."

He remembered his original visit as if it had happened only yesterday. Nothing in his life would ever match the wonder he felt upon seeing dozens of alien species going about their ordinary alien lives or the sleek, glass skyscrapers that cut through the upper atmospheres. His brain had gone numb, like someone had hit the off-switch to keep his circuits from overloading. It was a miracle he hadn't collapsed to the floor as a gibbering vegetable.

Now there was little remarkable about the scene before him, save for its, well, utter lack of anything remarkable at all. How normal a sprawling galactic community of unimaginable races had become in so short a span of time. Technologies and peoples beyond humanity's wildest dreams, and now they too were part of that community... or would be soon, provided mankind survived its second extinction event in as many years. Typical Earthling luck, Jack supposed. We escape a dying sun only to rock up in a neighbourhood set for extermination.

Both times thanks to the Prymalis, he reminded himself.

Instead of a bustling port full of pilots and passengers and, yes, a few subservient automata, he now faced a neglected dust bowl. A Drygg was piling his or her belongings into a crate nearby; the crane attached to their rusty miniature freighter waited to load it onto its open cargo bay. One of the nearby market stall owners, perhaps. A thin needle of a rocket stood upright half a dozen bays over, and a fluffy, feathery creature like a cross between Mardi Gras and a garden worm disembarked through a slitted doorway in its side... only to enthusiastically greet two more of its kind and eagerly invite them inside its ship to leave. A pair of metallic balls rolled through the dust towards a ship which sucked them, as if with magnets, into concave sockets on its wings. Whether the spheres were models of automata, some other kind of synthetic lifeforms, or simply ground transportation for smaller organic creatures was an answer quite beyond Jack's comprehension. His experience with the Nárva, coupled with the recollection of his first visit to Kapamentis, reminded him not to make any hasty assumptions.

"This district must be getting quiet," Rogan said as she joined them, "for the port's overseer to give up on this place."

"Or it's getting dangerous," Tuner suggested. "Kapamentis law enforcement used to be operated by the Ministry. I know Zsal and Heram said that essential services would continue to function for a while longer, but..."

"But we should be extra careful," Jack said. "Empty coffers get stretched thin pretty damn quick, and there are plenty of pirates willing to take advantage of the panic."

They left the port through the scrap metal doors. Rogan pointed out a broken mag-lock hanging off one of the handles. The owner hadn't just left the site unattended; outsiders had smashed their way in. Why somebody would break into an empty port was anyone's guess – maybe the owner had left a spare ship behind, too – but now the parking bays were open to everyone.

Jack shook his head. If this part of town was deteriorating so quickly, he could only imagine what Tortaiga Square was like...

"Hey, Adi." He spoke into his data pad. "Keep an eye out for anyone dodgy. There may be a few ship thieves about, especially with people growing so desperate to get off-world in favour of somewhere less populated."

"Will do," the *Adeona* replied. "If anyone tries to steal me, they're in for a nasty surprise. But I'll keep you updated in the event I have to relocate."

"Thanks, Adi. Speak soon."

Setting off through the market, Jack was stunned by how

few of the stalls remained. Upon his first and all subsequent visits, he could scarcely move without squeezing through crowds of scurrying Scrap Rats, inhaling the odours of a thousand exotic fruits and meats, or bumping into a disgruntled Ubekian Cutworm. There was no day and night cycle on Kapamentis, nor the concept of a weekend – any given minute on the city-planet was as busy as any other, regardless of which cultural or religious holidays might be celebrated from one day to the next. It was all that was brilliant and awful about the most bustling metropolis in the entire galaxy... and now it more closely resembled the aftermath of a music festival.

Though glad that fewer lives might be lost should the Prymalis attack go ahead, Jack hated that fear alone would strip the galactic community of its cultural synergy long before the enemy got there.

The Ministry headquarters was only a dozen streets away, at an intersection where the slipshod bustle of the market gave way to the high-rise towers of corporations, embassies and guilds. As they crossed from one side of the street to the other, a trash-truck came to sweep the litter from the gutters. Few vehicles patrolled the old streets anymore – wheels were horribly antiquated and there wasn't much use in a hover-car that couldn't reach the upper storeys of even the shoddiest neighbourhoods – and the way it belched and hiccupped as detritus funnelled into its gluttonous metal belly only furthered the impression of a city being dragged backwards. Holographic advertisements continued to bleat from towers above in neon blues, greens and yellows, obliviously selling pharmaceuticals and cybernetics to an audience who were only present because they couldn't afford, financially or emotionally, to leave Kapamentis for someplace else. Rain, an eternal presence, fell even harder than usual and smoke, normally dispersed by the constant buffering of air traffic, received the respite necessary to form dark grey cumulus clouds.

Perhaps he was finally seeing Kapamentis for what it always was, Jack wondered – a bleak, dark world crushed under its accumulated crud and despair. Or maybe this was just the face of a world at war... a war it had already lost.

"It's times like these," he muttered to the others, "I wish we still had something with which to defend ourselves."

"Yes," Tuner replied. "Even a Raklett rifle would do."

"Calm down, the both of you." Rogan shook her head; collected raindrops sprayed in every direction. "Look at this place. There's hardly anyone to defend ourselves against."

"Exactly." Jack peered anxiously down each side-alley they passed, certain he could see the goggle-glint of raiders who would never normally venture this far out from the rougher neighbourhoods. "It's the lack of crowds that worries me."

"Hmm." Whether Rogan shared Jack's paranoia or not, her pace noticeably increased. "Well, it's not far to the Ministry now."

They arrived at the foot of the Ministerium's steps only a few minutes later, mercifully untroubled by any unsavoury types lurking in the city's growing shadows. A handful more pedestrians shared the pavements with them, though the majority were glumly hurrying from doorways to impatient shuttles and taxi-pods rather than excitedly sampling the infinite opportunities normally available to citizens and tourists alike. Casting his eyes up to the ever-night sky, Jack was certain fewer casinos drifted across the stratosphere like flamboyant moons. Were they capable of skipping into different systems in search of more affluent clientele? He couldn't spot the Celest Verte anywhere.

"Less than a week since they shut the doors, and look at the state of it." Tuner waddled up to the steps and pointed at the piles of rubbish and squiggles of phosphorescent graffiti. "People have no respect."

"I hardly think many people had respect for the Ministry at the best of times," Rogan said. "Now there's nobody around to stop them from making their feelings known, that's all."

"People are scared," Jack said. "They're hearing terrifying stories about planets being destroyed and cultures wiped out. The Ministry has shut down and there's nobody to tell them what's going on or what they should be doing. Is it any wonder some people are losing their minds a little?"

"That's a very generous perspective to take," Rogan replied with a sardonic smile, "when it could just as reasonably be said that organics make a habit of destroying things as soon as they're let off the leash."

"Yeah, you're right." Jack raised an exhausted eyebrow. "I guess I'll go back to being the cynical one, shall I?"

The black pyramid of the Ministerium burgeoned before them, cold, withdrawn and uninviting. Jack shivered. Sandwiched between four giant pillars of obsidian, the deserted building suddenly resembled an ancient emperor's tomb.

"Shall we?" Tuner asked uneasily.

They climbed the concourse and unlocked the Ministry's doors.

6

MASS ADDRESS

Jack had considered the Ministerium deserted last time, when only a receptionist, physician and two Grand Ministers were in attendance. Compared to the lobby that presently greeted them, their previous visit was a goddamn rave.

The lights were switched off, as were the screens that normally showed either a live feed from inside the Ministerium chamber or various news broadcasts from across the galaxy. Jack thought that perhaps they'd crackle to life upon their group's presence, but no such luck. He switched on the flashlight attached to his suit and, running a hand through his lank, rain-soaked hair, wished he'd chosen to wear his cramped yet gadget-heavy helmet.

"We should be grateful that no pirates or raiders got inside," Tuner said, cooing at the empty hall. "They trashed some of the ancient Libraries just for fun. Imagine the damage they'd do to something actually owned by lawmakers."

"I'm sure it's just a matter of time," Rogan said. "Presuming the Prymalis don't destroy it first, of course."

"Hey, you never know." Jack shrugged. "They built this place, didn't they? Maybe they'll leave it standing – a keystone from which to rebuild their old civilisation."

"Oh, that's very reassuring." Rogan tutted. "So long as this building survives – not what it represents – that's all that matters."

"It was only a joke, Rogan."

"I know. I'm just not finding much humour in things at the moment."

The thuds of their footsteps echoed through the emptiness. With the doors shut behind them, all was utterly, eerily silent. No patter of rain outside, no hushed conversations between ministers dashing down hallways, no whirring and bleeping of electronics underneath the wide, barren desk. Only a stifling stillness that weighed even heavier upon them than the squatting darkness.

Yep. Jack nodded to himself. Definitely like a tomb. And galactic democracy was the corpse buried inside it.

Something moved above them. Jack spun around and shone his flashlight incriminatingly. But it was only one of the wayward blocks drifting across the Brutalist landscape, building corridors and barricading others as if possessing minds of their own. The interior of the Ministerium – designed by the Prymalis – continued to operate without the headquarter's regular power supply, Jack presumed. Even so, the grey cubes seemed to move more lethargically than usual.

Rogan, who hadn't been the remotest bit surprised by the meandering blocks, peered over the top of the reception desk. Nobody and nothing waited for her on the other side. The storage drives had been retrieved for storage elsewhere; even the filing cabinets containing what little physical records the Ministry kept to hand were empty.

"Can't see a way to activate the primary power systems from here," Tuner said following a brief inspection of the servers.

"We probably don't need them, right?" Jack glanced hopefully at Rogan. "The keycard reader by the front door worked. With any luck, so will the one for the Ministerium chamber and then the comm system. I imagine they're all on different networks in case of emergencies."

"Dare I say it," Rogan replied, "but Jack is probably correct. We'd best try the chamber and then worry about resetting cores if it ever comes to that."

They climbed the steps. A fist formed in the pit of Jack's stomach and grabbed hold of his intestines. Something didn't feel right, and it wasn't just the haunting absence of Ministry employees. They were intruders, unwelcome in these hallowed grounds whether they had Zsal's data pad in their possession or not. They knew it; the building knew it. Even the familiar golden statue at the top of the stairwell, the same abstract icon stamped onto every credit in the galaxy, transformed in Jack's imagination from a symbol of peace, hope and unity into a shiny guardsman poised to strike them down.

Jack sidestepped the grand display of stars and planets, knowing it was only the dark that frightened him and hoping that neither of the automata noticed. He raised Zsal's data pad to the reader beside the chamber's main door. It beeped in the affirmative and disengaged the locks. Rogan quickly pushed it open. Jack allowed himself to feel a modicum of relief that the Grand Minister's pad still retained the necessary clearance level, then followed the others through.

Perhaps, for once in their lives, a task as simple as sending out a wide-range transmission would remain so.

"Take a look at that," Tuner said in awe. "Now *this* isn't a sight many automata get to see."

The council chamber dilated; a silver-blue shimmer rippled from top to bottom across the bubble-pods like moonlight reflecting off an outdoor pool. An almost unfathomable space capable of accommodating representatives from more than two hundred thousand species, collectives and empires, all facing inwards towards a narrow, central branch of a platform on which six glimmering thrones lay empty, not only improbable in scale (the chamber was far greater in size than the whole of the Ministry headquarters) but also in function – those who watched from the cubicles above did so without any fear of tumbling out of their chairs and into their viewing windows. Though still cast in shadows and without its usual drones beaming colossal holograms of speakers into the chamber's upper and lower hemispheres, there was a subtle but unmistakable hum of life inside the spherical auditorium.

"Down there." Conscious that neither Rogan or Tuner had been permitted inside the Ministerium chamber before, Jack pointed to the long, precarious platform extending from a ramped entranceway on the opposite side. "Those chairs are where the Grand Ministers usually sit. That's where we'll find the emergency broadcast system."

"I'll take your word for it," Rogan replied. "Do you know how we get down there from here?"

"I think so. Follow me."

Cascading passageways ran around the circumference of the chamber like the upper balconies of a theatre. Ministers and the occasional dignitary or other guest could enter their respective pod by way of a door in its rear. It should have taken them hours to cover such a great distance, yet within minutes they found themselves more than a quarter of the way around. Time and space, knotted together, expanding and contracting according to subjective need – just how the Prymalis liked it, apparently. They passed a great many other doors leading back out of the chamber, similar to the one through which they entered though often varying in shape and size. Jack was sorely tempted to open a couple and find out where in the Ministry – hell, where in the *galaxy*, perhaps – they led, but Rogan reminded him they had more pressing matters to attend to first.

"Hello?" Tuner cupped his hands to his speaker and called out into the empty chasm. "Is anybody there?"

"Quiet!" Rogan hissed at him. "If there *is* anybody else here with us, do we want them to know?"

"I don't know." Tuner shrugged, his head bowed low. "Maybe they could help us get the Mass Address system operational."

The echo of his voice endlessly ricocheted off the protuberant walls. They waited breathlessly for an answer, but none came.

"It's probably for the best," Jack said, patting Tuner reassuringly on the head. "We're not even supposed to have Zsal's data pad, remember? It's not like we're cleared to be here, let alone do what we came to do. It could get us arrested... you know, if there was anyone left to arrest us."

"Just trying to be useful," Tuner muttered to himself.

They continued around the backstage passageways in an awkward silence. Before long they reached the spot where the spit extended from the ramped entranceway and descended a series of adjacent steps. Jack suddenly stuck out his arm and stopped the others before they could wander out onto the exposed platform.

"God, I hope they didn't activate the security system

before they left," he said uncomfortably. "Last time some-body crept in here uninvited they got positively shredded."

Rogan shot him a furious look.

"And you only thought to mention the deadly counter-measures now?"

"It slipped my mind," Jack replied. "I only heard the end result over the phone."

"Bolts alive..."

"I think it was only activated manually, if that's any consolation?" Jack smiled apologetically. "I don't think they'd normally leave turrets on. Imagine the diplomatic disaster if a minister wandered into the wrong room by mistake."

"Yes, Jack," Rogan snapped, "but there aren't any minis-ters anymore, are there? A lot of good it'll do the galaxy if we get disintegrated before we put out the call for help."

Tuner clenched his little metal fists and strolled out into the open.

"Wait!" Rogan shouted, desperately reaching out to grab him.

He reached the midpoint of the spit and hunkered down into a cube shape in anticipation of the worst. No rotary cannons or fission turrets sprouted from inside secret panels in the walls. No disintegration grid beamed into life from the impossibly thin walkway. The three of them weren't suddenly trapped inside anti-gravitational forcefield bubbles while a strike force got dispatched with orders to execute them. Tuner's tinny footsteps continued to echo like the dripping of a rusty faucet – otherwise, all was still.

"Maybe it's just set to target organics," Tuner suggested.

"Thanks," Jack said, edging out to meet him. "You know I love it when you shatter my sense of well-being."

They walked down the long, narrow platform towards

the grand chairs situated on the bulbous protrusion at the far end. Jack tried not to look over the edge at the nauseatingly long drop, but looking up made his vertigo even worse. If he focussed on the pods to either side, he'd likely walk right off the edge, especially given the way they seemed to distort around him. So he kept his attention on the chairs ahead, and the outline of Rogan walking slightly ahead of him, and concentrated his mind on hoping the comm system was still operational.

As for actually *operating* it, well, he'd leave that to Tuner. He could probably hack into the thing even without Zsal's data pad, the little scamp.

A lone pedestal stood in the middle of the seats, dark and inert. Rogan took Zsal's data pad and tried to activate it. Meanwhile, Jack eyed one of the golden thrones with a mischievous swell of desire in his heart.

"Ah, what the hell," he said, dropping into it.

"I wouldn't get too comfortable, interloper," said a tired, croaky voice from the back of the chamber. "The new owners will be moving in soon."

Jack closed his eyes and swallowed hard, even as Rogan and Tuner spun around in surprise. Slowly, already certain of the intruder's identity, he rose from the throne.

"Or should I say the old ones," the Archimandrite said, splaying out his skeletal fingers in mocking triumph.

The cult leader had always looked on the anaemic side – his towering species possessed heads like the exposed skull of a jackal, the chalk-white torsos of starving scarecrows and gangly arms that stretched down to their knees. Yet now the Archimandrite was truly knocking at Death's door. He'd evidently survived the unexpected self-destruction of Tuner's mech suit back on XO-R15, but not by a healthy margin. His pale chest was black with scorch marks and red where the raw flesh had twisted and burned. Part of his cheek-bone had been sheered off in the explosion, so his snaggle-toothed jaw hung in a permanent yawn. As he shuffled and limped down the spit towards them, Jack noticed that the lunatic was missing two of the knotted fingers on his right hand.

"It's not over yet," Jack said with as much bravado as he could muster. "Some of the major empires are holding their own against the Prymalis. The war can still be won."

"The war has barely started, and you know it." The Archimandrite barked out a single laugh like a car backfiring. "You've seen but a fraction of their force."

"Says you," Tuner snapped from behind Rogan's leg. The Archimandrite let out a short, sharp snarl and clenched his one intact fist... then composed himself and continued to converse with Jack instead.

"If you truly thought anyone could stand against the old ones alone, you wouldn't hope to bring everyone to Kapamentis to fight them. That is why you're here, is it not?"

Jack glanced at Rogan, who shrugged. The Archimandrite had been a faithful servant of the Prymalis right from the start – or at least from whenever the founder of the First Diakonos had originally learned of the ancient race's continued existence. It hardly mattered if he knew what they knew. Not anymore.

"Billions will die if the Prymalis attack Kapamentis," Jack replied. "Is genocide really what you want? To serve as a slave instead of living free like everyone your masters are trying to kill?"

"Do not try to fracture my pride, interloper." The madman attempted a grin despite his dislocated jaw. "From the fires the forest grows anew. A necessary sacrifice. To be a true believer... to bring about the cleanse... is an honour—"

"What a load of bollocks," Jack shouted. "Your flock is dead and your temple is obsolete. Do you really think the Prymalis will want to keep somebody from the charred remains of our galaxy around when all this is done? Give it up. Can't you see they don't need you anymore? Stop worshipping a bunch of prehistoric nut-jobs who'll wipe you out as soon as look at you."

The Archimandrite came to a hobbling stop only half a dozen metres down the narrow platform from where the three of them stood, his face all of a sudden wrestling with itself, and for a second Jack actually believed something he said had gotten through to the cultist. But then he wheezed out a sickly cough and raised one of his few remaining accusatory fingers.

"If the gods will it, it shall be," he declared resignedly. "Go ahead, heretics. Send out your call for help. Bring all of your armadas here from across the galaxy – you only bring about the total eradication of your forces all the faster. Kapamentis will be reduced to a blasphemous husk in seventeen hours either way."

"Seventeen hours?" Rogan stepped forward in alarm. "Is that when the Prymalis plan to get here?"

"You knew the destination, not the timeframe?" The Archimandrite chortled as he tilted his scarred head. "My, the unbelievers are even less prepared for their judgement than I thought. But you believe now, don't you? You all do. Please, tell all who will listen what awaits them. I did not come to this sacred place to stop you. No, I came only to bring retribution upon *that* one's metal head."

His finger pointed straight at Tuner, who shrank further behind Rogan's leg. She sidestepped to block him, as did Jack.

"You're not getting anywhere near him," Jack said, "so

just turn around and limp out of here, all right? Find a nice spot to watch all the chaos you've wrought. We won't even try to get you arrested or anything, honestly. We've got bigger fish to fry."

"You think I fear the indignation of the unrighteous?" the Archimandrite snarled. "That one has butchered me, put a spear through the spokes of every Order plan. I need not permission from gods or heretics to claim my recompense."

From the folds of his charred, black skirt he drew a short, stubby plasma repeater. With sudden, terrifying certainty that the conversation was now over, Jack rushed forwards and tackled the frail figure to the floor. The Archimandrite pulled the trigger but the plasma bolt shot inches above Rogan's shoulder. She hurriedly ushered Tuner behind one of the sturdy chairs.

The plasma repeater flew from the Archimandrite's hand, skittered across the polished platform, and dropped off the edge into the depths of the chamber below.

The cult leader swung his mangled fist towards Jack and landed a hit square in the torso of his spacesuit. Though his suit absorbed most of the impact, Jack still felt the wind get knocked from his lungs, and stars bloomed in the night that quickly flooded his vision. He faintly heard Tuner shout something in alarm and then a pair of powerful clawed legs booted him backwards.

Jack rolled clumsily towards the chairs. Rogan rushed forward to help him get back onto his feet. The Archimandrite rose to one knee and snarled in pain.

"How did you get in here, anyway?" Jack coughed as he staggered backwards. "Some hidden sub-basement teleporter to and from XO-R15 nobody else knows about?"

"The back door, you stupid heretic." The Archimandrite

tried and failed to reset his jaw. "One doesn't work for the Ministerium for fourteen local cycles without learning how to trick the system."

Jack faltered. "You worked here?"

"To my eternal shame, yes." The cultist's chest violently hitched once, twice, then settled as he finally succeeded at drawing breath. "How was it you thought I first learned of the old gods' plans? Blind luck? All the signs were there in the records. Now move aside, fool. You stand in the way of destiny."

"If destiny means Tuner getting pulled to pieces, destiny will have to go through me."

The Archimandrite spat out a thick globule of black blood.

"You reap, you sow."

He tried to shove Jack to one side; Jack hooked his leg around the Archimandrite's in an effort to trip him over. This time the skeletal scarecrow grappled the circumference of Jack's head as he once more toppled to the floor like a felled oak. They hit the spit with a smack. Jack tasted iron flood his mouth, felt blood trickle from his split lip and run like treacle up his cheek.

Fingers like gnarly roots wrapped around his skull and began to squeeze.

Rogan delivered a piston-powered punch to the side of the Archimandrite's skull. It cracked with a nauseating *snap*. He rolled over, one of his hands still hooked around Jack's head, dragging him across so that Jack ended up straddling the Archimandrite's chest. Before he could even think of pushing himself away, Jack found himself smashing his fists into the madman's bony face instead.

"This could have been a galactic utopia," he gasped in

between punches. "Everything that's going wrong is because of people... like... you!"

His foe glared up at him through a bloody, broken face and distributed a stinging haymaker in return. Jack tumbled head over heels, a nasty purple bruise promising to blossom under his right eye. Furiously indignant, the cultist found his feet, but Rogan shoulder-barged him off the spit before he could fully steady himself.

The Archimandrite quickly grabbed the side of the slender platform with his one good hand and clawed ineffectively for purchase with the other. All of the piousness drained from his face, instantly replaced by an expression of pure, mortal panic.

"Help me up," he begged through a hollow wheeze. "Forget the tin can. I deserve to see the flowering of the future I seeded."

Jack shook his head as Tuner nervously crept up behind him.

"No. You don't deserve to see a future at all."

He stomped down hard on the Archimandrite's fingers. The leader of the Order of the First Diakonos howled in pain, relinquished his tired grip, and dropped into the endless darkness of the Ministerium.

"Let's hope he stays dead this time," Tuner said, peering over the edge. They listened for a final *thud*, but there wasn't one.

"We couldn't have saved him," Rogan said to Jack. "If we'd tried pulling him up, he would have just sent us tumbling over instead. Men like that never stop."

"I know. It's done." Jack tried and failed to suppress a shiver. "Now let's do what we came to do and get out of here."

Rogan took Zsal's data pad and presented it to the pedestal. A pristinely clear hologram beamed forth from its peak. Even with no ports through which to hack and override the system, Rogan had no trouble navigating the high-security interface and finding the Mass Address comm channel.

"It's ready whenever you are," she said to Jack. "Simply record what you want to say and then hit Broadcast."

"Oh, you want me to do it?" He shook his head. "Nobody paid any attention the last time I put out a call for help. What makes you think it'll be any different now?"

They both turned to look at Tuner.

"Go on, buddy," Jack continued. "If there's anyone who can convince all the empires in the cosmos to put aside their differences, it's you."

"You really think anyone will listen to an automata?" he asked, his head bowed.

"I think they'll listen to the voice of someone who truly believes what he's saying," Jack replied. "I can't think of anyone better."

"Neither can I," Rogan agreed.

Tuner glanced at each of them sheepishly, then approached the pedestal. The angle of the holographic interface lowered accordingly. He raised a tiny metal digit, hesitated, and then tapped the button to record.

"Honoured empires of the galaxy," he began. Once more he turned to his friends for reassurance – they hurriedly and enthusiastically gestured for him to continue. "Member species of the Ministerium past and present, free peoples of the outer systems, organics and synthetics. If you can hear this, I beg you to listen.

"The mysterious fleet that has been attacking your colonies and homeworlds belongs to the ancients, the precursors, whatever your species calls them, and they're plotting a course for Kapamentis. In seventeen hours this bustling metropolis will be transformed into a world of ash. This celebration of all that unites us, for better and for worse – painstakingly forged over the past millennia despite our many conflicts and differences – will be lost forever.

"Some worlds can defend themselves against a couple of these battleships. Others can't. But none can stand alone against the full force of the Prymalis threat. Only if every available armada works together do we have any hope of stopping them and preventing our entire galaxy's extinction."

Tuner paused for a moment, then continued.

"Kapamentis. Seventeen hours. Please come. I don't want any more planets to die."

He nervously hit Broadcast, then hunched into a cube as if scared of what might happen next. Jack crouched down and patted him on the back.

"Good job, buddy."

"Do you think anyone will reply?" Tuner anxiously asked Rogan. "Do you think anyone will come?"

"I don't know if the channel is set up for two-way communication," she replied apologetically. "Maybe. I suppose we'll see."

They each took up position on a golden throne and listened for an answer.

In the full two hours they waited, they didn't receive a response of any kind.

7

NEON RAIN

Kapamentis rain lashed against the neon-soaked sidewalks. Sirens blared above the clouds of smoke and steam. Jack shovelled another spoonful of noodles into his mouth.

"So we're screwed, then," Tuner said.

"Seems that way," Jack replied. He absent-mindedly stirred a chunk of unidentifiable protein around the swirling labyrinths of wispy udon in his bowl. "Might as well enjoy good grub while it still exists."

"Excuse me." Tuner flagged down the noodle stand's attendant. "Can I have a canister of motor oil, please?"

"Make that two," Rogan said glumly, her metal head in her hands.

The Luethian waitress returned with two canisters and a fresh bottle of beer. Jack watched in bemusement as the automata unscrewed the lids and tipped the funnels into the respective receptacles in their sides.

"I'll never understand why automata find that so refreshing."

"And I'll never understand why fleshies enjoy compromising their mental faculties," Rogan replied, nodding at Jack's beer, "as if they aren't diminished enough to begin with. And yet..."

They sat alone under the plastic awning of the small, purple-lit, street-side bar, eating and drinking and re-oiling as the world failed to go on by. People seemed to be fleeing the planet with even greater enthusiasm than upon their arrival. Jack had to wonder how many citizens of Kapamentis and the wider galaxy secretly tuned their personal comm systems to receive the Ministry's supposedly secure broadcasts – the dark streets had certainly adopted a somber, more fatalistic atmosphere since they sent out their call for help.

Or maybe Jack was just projecting. He didn't suppose it mattered. Kapamentis was doomed either way.

"Fifteen hours," he mused, "before all of this comes to an end."

The Luethian attendant overheard him, paused in the act of dumping a fresh batch of suspicious meats into one of her cooking pots, and then hurried out the back of the stall to make some calls.

"There has to be *something* we can do," Tuner said, slamming his empty canister onto their table in frustration. A small wave of what were meant to be vegetables sloshed over the side of Jack's bowl. "We can't just sit here waiting for the Prymalis to arrive."

Behind them, the flimsy shutter of the noodle stand came rolling down. The purple lights switched off seconds later, then the belching generator.

"There's no use in travelling to any more planets begging for allies," Jack said, fishing out the last of his food. "Everybody heard the message you sent out, and we've exhausted our contacts. Who would we even go see?"

"Maybe not every planet is doomed," Tuner said brightly. "The automata have successfully kept Detri a secret from organics for years now. Who's to say the Prymalis won't overlook it too?"

"It's not the worst idea in the world," Jack said with a sigh. "I can't say I look forward to an eternity hiding inside a synthetic sanctuary, but it's better than certain death out here."

"Hardly a long term solution though, is it?" Rogan asked. "Detri might have some food reserves brought in by the sentient ships who've joined its ranks, but if the rest of the galaxy gets wiped out those reserves will dry up pretty quickly. And let's not forget that it was the old Prymalis star maps in the Libraries where the automata discovered Detri in the first place. We shouldn't assume it'll stay secret for long."

"We could make a quick trip over there, though." Jack shrugged. "If the two of you want to see Tork and the gang one last time before everything truly goes to hell."

"Quick trip?" Rogan laughed. "Don't you remember our first trip to Detri from Kapamentis? Even with Adi's upgraded skip drive, it'll take us more than our remaining fifteen hours to get there. And whilst the idea of hiding from the war on Detri is an appealing one, I don't think it's right that we put out a call for help only to run away ourselves. Or maybe that kind of old fashioned thinking is foolish when faced with these sorts of odds."

The Luethian, swallowed from head to tow in a four-sleeved macintosh raincoat, sprinted out from behind the stand towards the inter-district transport shuttles hovering a hundred metres down the street.

"No, Rogan's right." Tuner sank further into his seat. "We can't stay on Kapamentis waiting for annihilation because

I'll lose my bolts. But Adi can't take us anywhere too far from here because we won't get back in time for all the fireworks, and there's nobody with any political influence left to go see anyway. So where *can* we go?"

They went back to studying the stormy city. A magnificent silver-grey barge of titanium and carbon composite coasted overhead as it climbed sluggishly out of Kapamentis's atmosphere, at which point it would make the jump to another (supposedly safer) star system. Full of refugees, no doubt. Some of the bladed corporate skyscrapers had gone dark, the lights in their windows extinguished and the giant vertical fans of the upper storeys grinding to a stop for the first time in centuries, while others continued to holler out noisy neon advertisements as if in dogged dismissal that anything in the galaxy was amiss. A pair of Scrap Rats scurried down the pavement opposite the noodle stand carrying between them what looked to be a stolen carburettor, and a lone Krolak staggered back the other way, drunkenly snarling to itself. Aside from them, and the occasional weird centipede that scuttled out of the overflowing sewer vents, the city blocks surrounding the Ministry headquarters were deserted. Jack found himself wondering if any of the pleasure resorts on Kapamentis were still operational – it might be their last chance to spend their remaining galactic credits before they lost all value entirely.

"New Terra," Rogan said, finally.

Jack nearly choked on his beer.

"What?"

"New Terra," Rogan repeated. "Humanity's new homeworld. I know you keep up with all the news coming out of there, even if you don't like to talk about it. They've exterminated all but the last few roaches and begun rapid construction of their new settlements. Unfortunate timing, given that everything is coming to an end. But yes, New Terra isn't far from here. We've enough time to get there and back and still have a few hours spare to spend on-world, if you wanted."

"Presuming the Prymalis don't get here early," Tuner said.

"Presuming the Prymalis don't get here late," Rogan replied with a shrug. "As the Archimandrite's slip of the tongue is all we have to go on, we may as well presume he's right."

Jack sat back and let the two automata bicker over the possibility that the Archimandrite was a stooge sent to feed them bad information. *New Terra*. Humanity had spent the past year fighting – and often losing to – a horde of killer bugs who'd wiped out the indigenous population. With the death of the bug queen, the planet finally belonged to them. Until now, he hadn't found a reason to visit.

Well, that wasn't true. There were plenty of reasons to go. But he'd only needed the one reason to stay away.

"What about Klik?" Jack asked. "Isn't there time to go visit her, make sure she's okay?"

"Not unless you plan to wave at her from the cockpit windows as we shoot past," Rogan replied. "And you know Klik wouldn't appreciate us turning up unannounced. She'll think we're babysitting her. If you really want to speak to her beforehand, do it via video on the way to New Terra."

"I tried calling her earlier. She didn't answer. That's why I'm worried."

"Oh, she's probably just on a transport ship escorting Paryxian refugees someplace safer. If Salyn had been hit, we'd have heard about it. Come on, Jack. You know there's one person you ought to go see above all others, if this truly is the end."

Jack groaned and buried his head in his hands.

"I think I'd rather face the Prymalis," he mumbled. "Okay, sure. Let's go see what humanity's been up to since we screwed up their plans for New Eden. I bet everyone will be *so* glad to see us. That okay with you, Adi?"

"I'll take any opportunity to stretch my thrusters, Captain," said the *Adeona*, who'd been tuned into the conversation via Rogan. "It sounds much better than waiting to be stolen in this cruddy port. When can I expect you to get back here?"

Jack casually glanced up and down the deserted district.

"Actually, is it all right if you come direct to us?"

"Here?" Rogan asked incredulously. "You want Adi to land in the middle of the street?"

"Why not? Look at this place – it's not as if anyone's going to clamp her. Besides, I've got a beer to finish. Where we're headed I'm gonna need all the courage I can get."

8

NEW TERRA

The idyllic green and blue orb that was New Terra – known formerly as Ennakis by the previous (and now extinct) inhabitants, the Essyen – evoked swells of nostalgia and belonging Jack didn't expect. Though all of the jumbled oceans and continents were unrecognisable to any visitor from Earth, there was something about New Terra that truly felt like home.

And just as Earth had been orbited by a fine cloud of man-made detritus in the last of its dying days, so too was New Terra surrounded – this time, however, by comm satellites and Ark ships and UEC battlecruisers. It was something of a relief to see so many of the Arks floating lazily around the conquered planet – although Admiral Blatch had once told Jack of the project's success prior to their mission on New Eden, it was another thing entirely to see the evidence with his own eyes.

"Bolts alive," Rogan said as they viewed the UEC fleets from the cockpit. "There are quite a few more of you than when we last paid your species a visit."

"Yeah, we're a prolific bunch," Jack replied with a wry

smile. "Give us a few decades and there'll be even more humans than there were roaches."

"A few decades?" Tuner waddled up to join them. "They'll be lucky to have a few hours the way the Prymalis attacks are going. We need to get down to that planet and then back to Kapamentis, pronto."

Unfortunately, freely piloting the *Adeona* down to the surface of New Terra was not an option. Aside from the fact that New Terra was officially under military control while human society re-established itself, few people planetside (outside of top brass and designated traders and emissaries) had ever seen an alien before. That the crew aboard the *Adeona* consisted of one human and two automata was irrelevant – for all anyone on the ground knew, bloodthirsty tentacled beasties might come screaming out to kill everyone as soon as the airlock door was open.

They pinged out a message explaining the intention of their visit as soon as they entered New Terra's star system, drifted inertly around the planet until they received a response from the UEC. Their request to land was approved, though not before various frantic messages were sent up and down the chain of command, and they were instructed to follow a *Sparrowhawk* attack ship down to the designated landing site. Jack had little doubt that Admiral Blatch was at least partially responsible for the relatively quick clearance, unless tales of his own cosmic escapades had spread quicker than he thought.

The attack ship led the *Adeona* down past vast fields of swaying wheat, over lush green valleys and vales that crested and fell for as far as Jack's eyes could see, along bubbling brooks and barbarous rivers that cut through craggy shores like turquoise anacondas. Even Rogan and Tuner, who'd each seen more of the galaxy than Jack could imagine, appeared captivated by the view. Small birds flew amongst the clouds, but few animals roamed the land, most having been rendered extinct alongside the indigenous population by the bugs.

The genesis of a city appeared on the horizon. Its skyline was more construction crane than skyscraper, more quiet English town than bustling metropolis. At present it consisted of the mandatory United Earth Collective government building – a squat rotunda capped with a pretentious, columned dome not totally unlike that of the US Capitol Building or St. Paul's Cathedral back on Earth – a few unimaginative tower blocks that housed the scores of essential workers already brought down from the Arks, a modest district of rustic, old-world structures adopted by those selling their limited wares to those planetside, scattered temporary pre-fab huts and a sprawling favela of military tents and outposts.

New London. With the bug war officially over, each UEC nation state was permitted to begin construction of their respective cities, with many electing to name their sites after capitals back home. The majority of citizens aboard the three Arks from the United Kingdom would reside in New London once the basic amenities were finished, though plans were already underway to establish a second settlement to the north nicknamed New Edinburgh.

Tiny, scrappy, unfinished... and still Jack felt a throb of pride in his heart.

Though New London was surrounded by bountiful plains (and cleaved in half by a winding, imperial river which early residents had unimaginatively yet heartwarmingly christened the Thames), there was only a single site suitable for incoming spacecraft – the same open-air hangar used by the UEC military for jet fighters and drop ships.

Humanity's introduction to the wider extra-terrestrial community was a drip-fed process, with half of mankind still dismissing the existence of other intelligent species as nonsense and conspiracy. Previous interactions between the UEC board members and Ministry representatives such as Grand Minister Heram had taken place in private battle-cruiser hangars, and any trade conducted with alien outsiders was done by specialist teams on minor planetoids far from civilian eyes. There was too great a risk of wide-spread panic amongst an already anxious population, espe-cially after the distressing and grisly events of the past year. Anyone wishing to visit a settlement – human or not – needed to go through a more resilient (not to mention well-armed) demographic first.

Still, the *Adeona* garnered plenty of attention from stationed marines as she settled into a landing position on her designated bay. She was most likely the first non-human-built ship to visit New London – the whole planet, for all they knew. Though the automata had reached out to humanity soon after they arrived at New Terra – machines who could think, talk and walk were easier, apparently, for the baffled Earthlings to accept – they were medical units mostly consigned to the Arks and battlecruisers in orbit. Soldiers up in the watchtowers stared in amazement as Adi descended on her secondary thrusters, her shielded, indus-trial mining hull a far cry from those of the inferior, mass produced tin cans to which the marines were accustomed – some of which Jack may have even helped assemble in the Pits back at Sandhurst all those relative years ago.

Jack stopped the two automata at the top of the *Adeona's* loading ramp before it opened. The last time they came to visit humanity, Rogan and Tuner (and Klik – *especially* Klik) had needed to remain on board and out of sight while First (official) Contact was made. Fourteen months made a world of difference, but he didn't want to encourage any of the greener marines' trigger fingers.

"Stay behind me and let me do the talking, okay?" he said apologetically. "I'm not trying to keep you hidden, or silence you or anything, just, you know..." He gave up. "Humans can be idiots."

"Oh, we're well aware of that," Rogan replied with a wink.

The loading ramp descended. A four-strong fireteam waited for them at the bottom, nervously clutching their rifles. Jack felt his guts somersault at the sight of them. Witnessing human beings out in the wild was still a novelty, even for a fellow Earthling.

"Jack Bishop?" the sergeant asked. "And the automata —" he double-checked his data pad "—erm, Rogan and Tuner?"

"That's us, sir," Jack replied. Behind him, Rogan smiled politely; Tuner offered a little wave.

"And it's just the three of you, is it?" The sergeant kept glancing between the two robots and the dark maw that was the *Adeona's* cargo bay. "You don't have any other, erm, *entities* on board?"

"Nope, just us," Jack said with a shrug. "Feel free to take a look around if it makes you more comfortable. Just don't touch anything. The ship won't like it."

They left the sergeant to contemplate the implications of that last sentence as a second fireteam escorted them out of the bay and down the steel steps into the wider compound. More marines clustered to either side of them, their assignments forgotten, watching in confusion, awe or both as the two automata strolled innocently past, each wondering what all the fuss was about.

"Some of them look the same as you did the first time we brought you on board the *Adeona*," Tuner whispered to Jack. "Like a formipod has peed in their water tank."

"When I left Earth, we didn't have androids *or* proper artificial intelligence," Jack replied, avoiding everyone's gaze. "Imagine people's surprise at seeing both at once."

Rogan smiled as she studied the rows of bewildered faces.

"So primitive," she said affectionately. "Barely more advanced than Rakletts…"

"Hey." Jack nudged her with his elbow. "That hurts."

Their silent chaperones led them down a narrow path of rotten boards flanked by three-metre chainlink fences. Large command tents stood in the mud to either side, as did tanks and transporters and all manner of different utility vehicles. Jack could tell from the uninspiring tower blocks and herd of construction cranes poking over the compound's exterior perimeter that they were headed towards the true, more permanent settlement.

The sergeant in charge of the fireteam barked for the marines stationed beside the gates to open them. As they rumbled apart on their tracks, Jack spotted a pair of silhouettes leaning against a crumbly stone wall on the other side. They straightened up and dusted off their fatigues as the crew approached and the accompanying fireteam fell back.

One of the figures stuck out a high-tech prosthetic hand. Jack gave it an alarmed double-take before clasping it enthusiastically in his own.

"Bloody hell, Ginger. What happened to your arm?"

"A hug bit it off, obviously." His daughter rolled her eyes. "What else?"

An awkward silence divided them. Tuner waved energetically at Duke, who lurked behind Ginger like a smiley nightclub bouncer. Jack tried to swallow and discovered his throat was as tight and dry as the pinched neck of an hourglass.

"You remember that drink we promised to catch up over?" he said. "I think we ought to get it now."

———

THE FIVE OF THEM – Jack, Ginger, Rogan, Tuner and Duke – occupied the only pair of repurposed army canteen tables outside a pub set up inside the half-derelict shell of an old, stone Essyen townhouse. Other local establishments included a food market offering local fruits and synthetic meats, a small boutique selling (and repairing) leather shoes and beige outerwear, and a pharmacy-surgery hybrid for remedying the locals' non-life-threatening ailments. A water fountain sporting the broken lower half of an indigenous figure of legend lay dry and dusty in the centre of the courtyard.

Three pint-mugs of beer were slammed onto the table by the bartender.

"Here's to winning the war," Duke boomed as he raised his tin mug, "and starting a new chapter in humanity's story."

"Cheers," Jack said, timidly clinking his own against Ginger's.

They drank deeply. Rogan and Tuner sat on the bench opposite, fascinated – not at the mundane act of consuming alcohol (Jack had given them more case studies of that than the automata cared to count), but rather at the complex intricacies of inter-human interaction. The last time they got the chance to study it in any depth, everyone had been a little too preoccupied with preventing the UEC's unlawful genocide of the Flo'wud on New Eden.

Jack wiped his upper lip with the back of his hand and hoped someone else would kickstart the conversation. Every time he thought of a word to say it sprouted claws and anchored itself halfway up his throat. Ginger – real name Elizabeth Rogers – was his biological daughter, but his wife Amber had brought her up alone after Everett Reeves "accidentally" shot him through time and space and everyone presumed him dead. He hadn't even known Amber was pregnant when he left. In the almost thirty years Ginger had been alive, Jack had only spent a couple of days with her. Where was he supposed to start?

"New London is coming along well, I see," he just about managed.

"Hell yeah, it is," Duke replied with a triumphant grin. "Ain't it amazing what people can achieve when everyone pulls together? Especially when the alternative is living in those tiny coffin bunks up on the Arks."

"Workers' digs are mostly done," Ginger added casually. "Then it'll be the fancier condo towers, then hospitals and such and such, you get the picture. It's pretty boring work, to be honest. I'll take it over fighting those damn bugs any day, though."

"You can say that again," Duke said, absent-mindedly rubbing his shoulder.

"When is everyone else coming down from the Arks?" Jack asked.

"Some time yet," Ginger replied. "The hydro-electric dam is almost operational, but we've got a long way to go before New London is more than just a slab of mud and concrete. Better for civvies to stay in orbit until the amenities are better down here than up there. Plus there are all sorts of labs and data centres on the Arks that'll be too expensive to replicate planetside for a while."

"Maybe they'll land them one day," Duke wondered aloud. "I mean, why not? The Arks took off from Earth, didn't they? Easier to repurpose them as fancy skyscrapers than leave them all floating up in space."

"Not sure how that would work." Jack shook his head. "The centrifugal design of the exterior barrel only functions when..."

He trailed off when he realised everybody was staring at him in befuddlement.

"But yeah, maybe," he concluded, going back to his drink. "Gotta do something with them, I suppose."

"So. Jack Bishop." Ginger crossed her arms and leaned across the wooden table to face him. "I can't say I wasn't surprised when word came through you were visiting New Terra. There I was thinking you chose to leave humanity behind for good. I'm guessing you didn't come to talk urban design, so what really brings you to our neck of the woods?"

"Right, let's leave them to it." Duke snatched up his drink and gestured for Rogan and Tuner to follow him. "This is gonna be awkward enough without us lot listening in. Besides, I need to know how *you* came to be so small..."

"Well," Tuner said brightly as he hopped off the bench, "that's a long story involving a mech suit and a big explosion..."

"Sounds like my favourite kind," Duke said, winking.

Jack waited until the others were out of earshot, took a long swig of his own beer, tried not to wilt under heat of Ginger's inquisitive stare, and then finally summoned the courage to speak.

"I'm sorry it's taken so long for me to come," he mumbled. "First there was the mess on New Eden, then there was the bug war, and... well... I wasn't sure you'd even want to see me."

"Uh huh." Ginger raised an incredulous eyebrow. "And what changed?"

Jack tapped his finger against the table.

"There is a degree of, erm... *turbulence* in the galactic community," he said, bobbing his head to either side. "I don't know how much the UEC tells you – presuming the UEC knows anything at all – but things are getting pretty bleak out there. A few of us have tried to stop what's coming, but, well, humanity might get caught up in it too. I wanted to, you know, clear things up between us before it does."

"Pfft. There's always something." Ginger drank. "Can't be any worse than the roaches, can it?"

"Oh, you have no idea. This time it's our turn to be exterminated."

Ginger froze with her drink pressed to her lips.

"That bad? Really?"

"Yep, that bad." Jack went to finish his beer, found his mug empty. "Sorry to forever be the bearer of bad news. It seems humanity can't catch a break."

Ginger raised her mechanical arm and clicked her metal fingers together.

"Two more beers, please," she shouted to the bartender. "And make them the strongest you've got on tap."

Jack regaled Ginger with the story of the Archimandrite and the First Diakonos, of his voyage to the dark extroplanet XO-R15, of the eventual discovery of the Prymalis and their twenty-seven thousand year plan culminating in the eradication of all intelligent life in the galaxy. They were both two-thirds of the way through their second pint by the time he reached the point where the crew of the *Adeona* chose to make the trip to New Terra.

"So we're buggered, then." Ginger laughed. "For Christ's sake. I'm starting to think I should have stayed on Earth."

"You and me both. At least then I wouldn't have lost..."

Jack caught himself. It was easy to forget who he was talking to. For all the years he'd loved Amber – and he knew he forever would – he couldn't wrap his head around the fact that Ginger had actually known his wife for longer.

"Look, Ginger..." He resisted the urge to reach across the table and clasp her hands in his own. "I'm so, so sorry. If I'd known your mother was pregnant with you, I never would have volunteered for that damn stupid experiment. Things were desperate, you see. I wish I could—"

"It's okay, Jack." Ginger raised her hand as her face stiffened. "You don't need to apologise. I read through the reports. You couldn't have known you were signing up for a one-way trip."

"Even so." Jack's shoulders sagged. "The thought of leaving Amber behind to bring you up by herself... of not being a father to you while you were growing up in an already grave world... Christ Almighty. Makes me feel sick just thinking about it."

"Stop. Just..." Ginger closed her eyes and turned away. "It's not your fault. There's no use in dwelling on what you can't change. From what I saw on New Eden, from what you just told me about trying to stop the Prymalis... I know you're a decent guy, Jack. Hell, it sounds like you're almost as big a hero as the guys and girls who fought down here. Yeah, we both lost something when you disappeared that day – me a father, you a daughter. But for Christ's sake, stop blaming yourself. I don't. Mum sure didn't."

Jack smiled mournfully.

"Your mother. There are decades I missed. Tell me how you remember her."

Ginger opened her mouth as if to protest, then softened. She could tell how much he needed this.

"Smart. Caring. A wit sharp enough to cut through even the most spiteful teenage outburst." She tilted back on her bench in thought. "Beautiful, with tumbling auburn hair and a smile light the brightest dawn. And she was as strong and stubborn as a great oak, right up until the end."

"Ha! Yeah, that was Amber, all right." Jack downed the rest of his beer. "Man, I only hope I have half her strength in the day ahead."

9

ZARVU GAMMA

Proton charges tore across the amaranthine sky of Zarvu Gamma. The fifth herd of the Alpha Rhoden ground surge stampeded into the closest trench before one of the charges shot down like a dropped cannonball and eviscerated the stellated dodecahedral command centre half a klick to their rear.

The komanda shielded her beady black eyes from the mushroom cloud.

"Looks like we're on our own, girls," she grunted to her troops.

Hulking, spiny Prymalis stomped across the mud plains towards the capital city of Coryum. The westerly rain silos had already been atomised, as had the nuclear generators – the same fate could not await the Alpha Rhoden barricaded inside the city, no matter the cost.

"Why's these freaks even down here?" a member of her herd shouted over the din of laser fire and crackling electrostatic hisses. "Didn't they blast Paryx from outside the atmosphere?"

"It ain't our job to ask questions," the komanda replied, "just to kill 'em."

Of course, had the Alpha Rhoden been privy to the same knowledge as Jack and the crew of the *Adeona*, they would have known that the Prymalis needed to leave the majority of planets unspoiled less their self-imposed exile to let the galaxy regrow be for nothing.

But the fifth herd had more immediate concerns.

A projectile from the advancing forces screamed over the plains and blew a seismic crater in the lignite bedrock a mere half a dozen metres ahead of them. Dirt sprinkled over those hunched inside the trench, who each raised a horned head in almost reverent gratitude. They normally paid good credits for such a service back in their home-towns. The stench of burned ozone filled their slitted nostrils.

"Second and fourth herds are dead," the komanda grunted. "Third herd is scattered, unable to regroup under heavy suppressing fire. Sixth and seventh herds are on their way from Coryum, but they ain't gonna reach us for another eighth of a cycle. We can't let any of these outsiders past us."

"What about the Nashyngur?" somebody asked.

"Does it sound like the Nashyngur are holding them back?" the komanda replied, ducking as another proton charge went off.

Far ahead, beyond the last of the trenches, a division of male Alpha Rhoden warriors dressed in full carbyne armour with six-foot blades strapped to the insides of their arms waded through the invaders. Craggy Prymalis spines and limbs went flying. But whilst carbyne appeared to provide a limited degree of resistance to the enemy's disinte-gration weaponry, the sheer number of Prymalis ground troops was making short work of the elite (and blood-mad) Nashyngur.

"Horns down," the komanda's second-in-command said, peering through the cloud of debris. "We've got incoming!"

A Prymalis attack ship screeched out of the brown mist, skimming only a few metres above the mud plain. Its ballistic turrets opened fire. One of the Alpha Rhoden soldiers at the top of the trench exploded against the ridge opposite in a splatter of pinks and purples.

"Bombers!" the komanda bellowed. "Up front!"

Three particularly muscular Alpha Rhoden stomped forwards. Plasma cannons were strapped onto their backs and their eyes were protected by telescopic goggles. They snorted and dug their elephantine feet into the dirt.

"Hold..." the komanda instructed. "Hold..."

The attack ship continued to bombard the trench, the scream of its supersonic flight growing louder and higher in pitch. The Alpha Rhoden barely flinched, save for the click and whir of the Bombers' goggles locking onto their target.

"Staggered launch!" the komanda roared. "Release now!"

The three Bombers fired their cannons one after the other – centre, left, then right. Each skidded backwards through the mud from the force of the blast. The orbs of plasma soared through the sky towards the attack ships, which dodged them with transparent ease. Yet the komanda smiled. The orbs looped around and chased the Prymalis vessel back towards the trench. The ship banked right to avoid the first homing projectile, but the second and third reduced it to a chargrilled husk that skidded to a stop fewer than fifty metres ahead of the fifth herd's position.

"More," her second-in-command grunted as she

squinted through her own set of goggles. "Ugly louse-bugs on foot this time."

Prymalis foot soldiers continued hulking across the plains towards them, their stony black exoskeletons glistening under the burning sky. More than a few boasted scars from their run-in with the fallen Nashyngur. They opened fire on the trench the moment they came within killing range.

The Rhoden answered in kind with their own plasma rifles – no order from the komanda necessary. Another charge plummeted from the heavens and buried the northern end of the trench under half a kiloton of rock and nuclear fire. A dozen Alpha Rhoden were lost under the raining rubble. As many again died as Prymalis lasers transformed them into mists that quickly dissipated in the harsh Zarvu winds.

The komanda rose to full height, calmly peered through her rifle's holo-sights and gave the enemy a demonstration on how she became leader of the fifth herd. Each of the Prymalis required two hits to put down, she found, even when targeting their wide, overdeveloped heads. The first burned a hole through their hardened exoskeleton, the second their exposed organs. She estimated that four were dead by her hand before she was forced back into cover.

Her second-in-command was not so nimble. A blinding arc of crackling electricity only caught her on the leathery shoulder, yet in an instant she was nothing but a vapour drifting through their scattered ranks. The komanda bellowed in frustration and reset her plasma rifle, ready for the next defensive barrage.

But there was to be no barrage. Six hours after the invasion of Zarvu Gamma began, all fell suddenly silent.

Curiously and carefully, the surviving Alpha Rhoden

stomped up the side of the trench and watched as all the Prymalis squid-ships slithered up towards their mothership in orbit. The only enemies left on the battlefield were dead.

"They're backin' off," one of the Rhoden grumbled, sheathing her rifle in disappointment. "Where do you think they're goin'?"

"No idea," the komanda replied. "I'm just glad it ain't here."

10

THE FINAL DAWN

Somebody cleared their throat behind Jack. He twisted around on his bench to discover a particularly stern-looking marine standing to attention behind him with his hands folded behind his back. He appeared to be staring at a construction crane far in the distance.

Jack struggled not to laugh at the idea that this man was pretending his tickly cough belonged to someone else.

"Mr. Bishop, sir," the marine barked. "Admiral Blatch requests your presence at once, sir."

"Did she specify where that presence needs to be?" Jack replied with a sheepish grin. He pointed to the table while Ginger buried her head in her hands. "Because I'm quite happy catching up with my daughter here, thanks."

The marine didn't so much as budge an eyeball in Jack's direction. In the resulting silence, Jack had a sudden suspicion that in the Admiral's vocabulary, "requests" was just a politer synonym for "demands".

"It's fine," Ginger said, raising her prosthetic hand. "I'd better be heading back, anyway. Just because I'm off-duty for the day doesn't mean I don't have a crap-tonne of stuff to be getting on with. And we wouldn't want to keep the Admiral waiting, would we, soldier?"

"No, ma'am," the marine replied, and Jack was sure he caught the faintest smirk cross the man's lips. Jack may have been a modest figure of legend for those who knew the story of Everett's wormhole experiments, but Ginger was one of humanity's very real heroes. The war against the roaches couldn't have been won without her. She commanded respect from privates and generals alike.

Jack and Ginger rose from the picnic bench, leaving behind four empty glasses of beer and a small basket of fries. Jack was enormously happy to discover that New Terran soil grew fantastic potatoes. At the same time, Duke escorted Rogan and Tuner around the cobbled path that circled the old Essyen townhouses. The Admiral's marine waited wordlessly for everyone to say their goodbyes.

"I guess this is it, then," said Ginger, walking around to Jack's side of the table. "If everything out there is as bad as you make out, we may never see each other again."

She smiled and brushed her purple fringe out of her eyes. Jack was suddenly struck by their similarity to Amber's. Hadn't he ever noticed that before?

"Try not to get yourself killed." She extended her hand of flesh and bone. "You're a good drinking buddy. And there's nobody else who knew Mum."

He gripped her hand in his own, shook it a few times, and resisted the urge to pull her in for a hug. Ginger didn't seem the hugging type, and his brain was full with too many conflicting emotions.

"Nice to see you again, Mr. Bishop," Duke said, giving Jack a goofy yet earnest grin. "I brought your two friends back in one piece."

"We saw cows," Tuner said excitedly.

"It was... enlightening," Rogan added, using the wall of the fountain to scrape muck off her foot.

"Let's be off, then," Jack said to the marine standing to attention. "Ginger. Duke. Stay safe, all right?"

"Til next time, Dad," Ginger said with a wink.

Jack suffered an involuntary shudder.

"If I live past tomorrow, please just call me Jack."

"Yeah, it felt wrong even as I said it." She waved dismissively as she and Duke headed for the heart of New London. "Ciao."

ADMIRAL BLATCH WASN'T on New Terra. This shouldn't have surprised Jack. She was in charge of not only the *Final Dawn*, the Ark to which she'd been assigned as a Captain, but the United Kingdom's other two colony ships and a whole UEC fleet. In the year humanity had spent liberating the planet from the bugs, Blatch hadn't once stepped foot on it.

Jack was escorted back to the *Adeona*, where he received instructions to follow a *Sparrowhawk* gunship up to the *Final Dawn*. Whether it was the same ship that escorted them down to New London, he didn't know. He simply collapsed into his captain's chair, relayed the order to Adi, and relaxed while they made the slow trek back into orbit.

Humanity's new world. Hundreds of cities cropping up across its surface like mushrooms come the fall. A whole species starting anew. And all of it wiped away in an instant should the Prymalis turn their sights on it.

He hadn't thought it possible for this fight to feel any more personal. Boy, was he wrong.

They were led by the *Sparrowhawk* to the same hangar

as when they first visited the *Final Dawn*. Jack couldn't tell one docking bay from another and presumed most hangars on the Ark were based on the same design, but Adi's memory was infallible. As the Ark used blast doors rather than forcefields, the marines stationed there were tethered to the floor and kitted out in full cosmonaut gear. The *Adeona* landed where she was told, the giant blast doors rumbled across their tracks again, and air was pumped back into the hangar. When the klaxon stopped wailing outside the ship, a strike force of black-clad marines entered via security tunnels and circled the ship.

Jack sighed. It was obvious a conversation with the Admiral would be expected should he ever return to human-occupied space, but seeing first-hand all that humanity might lose hadn't exactly left him in the right mood. And they really needed to be leaving – the *Adeona* barely had enough time to get back to Kapamentis before the Prymalis were due to arrive as it was.

"Hopefully I won't be long," he told Rogan and Tuner as he left the cockpit. "The Admiral is probably just fishing for intel on humanity's new neighbours."

"Or she wants to arrest you," Tuner suggested, "following an official investigation into the events of New Eden."

"Don't get yourself locked up," Rogan said absent-mindedly. "We're still leaving, with or without you."

"Fine by me." Jack shrugged. "Better to rot in a UEC jail cell than face the Prymalis anyway..."

He descended the open loading ramp, surprised by how unperturbed he was by all the assault rifles pointing in his direction. Without his spacesuit, a single shot could kill him. Even with his spacesuit, perhaps. He didn't fancy finding out. But funnily enough, he found himself more concerned with being criminally underdressed for his meeting than anything else. He'd worn his smartest clothes for his meeting with Ginger, though his wardrobe was rather limited, and the same would have to be good enough for the Admiral.

"This way, please," said the marine closest to the ramp, and the group immediately escorted him towards a security door at the rear of the hangar. Jack hoped that the word "please" meant incarceration was off the table, though the following terminology the marine grunted into his comm unit to co-ordinate his arrival made Jack sound more like an asset than a human being.

From the UEC's perspective, he supposed that's what he was. A former employee (read: property) who disappeared during an official experiment and was likely now humanity's greatest link to the wider alien community. A very precious asset indeed.

Through the security door was an array of elevators, though, given the Ark consisted of a barrel-shaped exterior rotating around a central, vertical strut, they were just as likely to travel sideways as up and down. Jack recognised them from his previous visit.

"You can drop me off here, guys," Jack said. "If we're headed to the Admiral's office, I think I remember the way."

"No can do, Mr. Bishop," another marine replied. "You're our charge til you're in her company."

"And we ain't going to her office," a third marine growled.

Jack gulped. Perhaps jail was an option, after all.

He was ushered into one of the elevators; the marines filled all the available space around him. It shot off with a press of a button – upwards in regard to the overall ship (in other words, towards the upper floors and parallel with the top of the central strut), yet sideways from the perspective of everyone inside the elevator cabin. Jack had grown too accustomed to artificial gravity generators – he struggled to wrap his head around a centrifugal system where down could theoretically mean two directions at once.

This was technology from the 2070s retrofitted into a ship constructed in the late 2030s and early 2040s. The elevators and shuttles hadn't the velocity of those in the average Kapamentis skyscraper, let alone an outpost in the Mansa Empire. It took a minute and a half to reach their destination and nobody uttered a word in the meantime. When their cabin rumbled to a stop, the doors opened with a familiar *ping* noise.

"Right this way, sir," the first marine said, hurrying Jack out of one elevator and into another right beside it – another marine, sans black visor, stood holding it ready for them. This time the elevator acted traditionally, rising only a single storey within the band in which they'd arrived before its doors *pinged* open again. Once more Jack was ushered out without explanation. All but one of the remaining marines positioned themselves around the white, plasticky lobby.

"Where the hell are we?" Jack muttered to himself.

"Platinum Sector," his escort answered, much to Jack's surprise. "It's the band where the richest passengers live," he explained, sensing Jack's confusion. "Not those who won tickets in the lottery, you know? The first lift took us to their suites. This here's the hospitality district."

Of course. Jack remembered the outrage when it was announced that the wealthy elite could buy their way onto a new world. Tickets cost tens of millions of dollars each – some families had spent billions securing their bloodline's survival. Jack and Amber hadn't been all that surprised.

How else did people expect the UEC to fund the construction of the Arks?

"Hospitality district. Huh. The apocalypse sure hit these guys hard, right?"

"I don't much care how this lot live," the marine replied dismissively. "They give me three hots and a cot. I'm just grateful to be alive."

Jack shut up. He'd forgotten the hell the rest of humanity had gone through to even get this far. Three hots and a cot was old prison-speak. When you're trapped on a ship with zero chance of a career change for the foreseeable future, he supposed there wasn't a huge lot of difference.

He was the one free to explore the galaxy in his own starship. If anything, the average person on board the Arks and UEC battlecruisers probably looked at *him* in contempt, not the snobs living just a few bands over.

As they passed through an automatic door, the sterile and clinical walls of the elevator lobby were swapped out for corridors panelled with dark, varnished wood. Paintings hung from the walls. Not even prints, Jack was alarmed to discover – actual *oil paintings from Earth*. He suspected the miniature chandeliers hanging from the ceiling were glass and electric, but still. Well-dressed men, women and children strolled through the halls, chatting and laughing as if they were waltzing down restaurant row. Only a few gave so much as a glance in the soldier's direction. Ever-present security was normalised.

"So this is where the elite eat and drink," Jack mused to himself. "Fascinating. Now I see why so many famous chefs got given tickets."

Signs for American steakhouses, Italian buffets and teppanyaki grills hung above classic wooden doorways, as did more than a few classic fast food chains Jack recognised from back home. And it wasn't just restaurants. Cafes modelled on French bistros and quaint English pubs (complete with artificial fireplaces) were present, too. For a second Jack wondered if he'd woken on a luxury cruise ship and everything up until this moment had been a dream.

"Excuse me," the marine said firmly to a slightly inebriated crowd which had gathered outside an Indian restaurant. "Coming through."

They arrived at some kind of bar or nightclub right at the back of the district. A tiny, barely visible plaque to the right of the dark, curtained doorway read *Spacebar*. Very original, Jack thought. There were no windows. Jack's escort stood at-ease outside the entrance.

"In you go," said the marine.

"Whose name is the reservation under?" Jack asked.

"Oh, I think you'll find your table easily enough."

Jack ducked under the plush, navy blue curtains and passed through a sparse cloak room. Nobody minded the desk. Already he could hear the faint twinkling of piano keys coming from behind the double doors ahead so, in lieu of any other option save for an employees-only office and a pair of bathrooms, he pushed them open.

Once more he felt transported back in time. How many years had it been since he stepped foot in a place like this? *Truly* like this, he meant. Sure, there were bars on Kapamentis, and indeed on most planets that had been colonised in some way or form. But their clientele were too diverse for anything – save for the shared intention of destroying organic brain cells, as Rogan so succinctly put it – to feel familiar. Nothing was ever designed with a human being in mind. And yet the *Spacebar*... it could have been shipped straight from Earth.

Hell, it was one of the first places he'd been in over a

year that had been designed with *only* human beings in mind.

Dozens of circular tables were laid out across a black carpet, each flanked by four wooden chairs. A grand piano occupied much of the stage to Jack's right, though a quick glance told him that nobody was playing it – the keys he heard were drifting softly from speakers nestled amongst the dim lights and shuttered vents in the ceiling. A relatively well-stocked bar lined the wall at the back, its mirror barely visible behind shelves of classic liquor, and a waistcoated bartender hurriedly – almost nervously – rearranged glasses behind a counter flush with bar stools. He was the lone visible employee, unless the two marines lurking in the corners of the room were also on the venue's payroll. The entire left-side wall, directly opposite the stage, consisted of floor-to-ceiling windows offering a staggeringly beautiful view of New Terra, though given the layout of the Platinum Sector's hospitality district (not to mention the risk of depressurisation should the glass crack) Jack suspected these were not actually windows but rather high-definition screens relaying footage captured from the ship's exterior. Still, it was damn enviable.

Sitting at one of the tables closest to the faux-window was Admiral Blatch. She nodded politely when she noticed Jack loitering in the doorway.

"Mr. Bishop," she said, gesturing to the empty place opposite her. "Come. Sit."

He navigated a path through the empty tables, suddenly self-conscious of the awkward way he walked, and pulled out a chair. The man from behind the bar was already standing beside their table before Jack's bum so much as brushed his seat's rather expensive-feeling cushion.

"What would you like, Mr. Bishop?" Blatch asked. "It's all on the house. Provided it's human-made, of course."

Put on the spot, Jack could hardly remember any brands from back on Earth. Kraken rum wouldn't have gone amiss. But instead he shook his head.

"Thank you, but I'd best not. Still got a hell of a long day ahead of me..."

"Suit yourself. I'll take a Moscow mule. It's not often I get a chance to 'hit the town' these days."

The bartender went to leave, only to hesitate when Jack suddenly perked up.

"Actually, I'll have an orange juice. Sorry, is that possible? Do you still grow them? Oranges, I mean. It's just I haven't had any Earth fruit since, well, you know..."

"Certainly, sir," the bartender said, unable to hide his amusement as he left. "Won't be a moment."

"Humanity can't go colonising a new world without vitamin C," the Admiral said, smiling. "I know this is a ship, but a scurvy outbreak in the twenty-first century might just be the last straw."

"Well... two hundred and ninetieth century or something, relatively-speaking."

"Yes, indeed! Baffles the mind, frankly. But that's all behind us, anyway. Meaningless old-world measurements, aren't they? Going forward everybody's to use the AE system. So, right now, we're two years After Exodus. Or 'After Earth', as I've heard some call it."

Good grief. Humanity wasn't even waiting to see how the rest of the galaxy functioned before coming up with its new calendar. Way to keep things simple, guys. Though Jack had to admit the Ministry's standardised system of impossibly long digital time codes wasn't any more relevant (or comprehendible) for a freshly reborn species than Earth's old anno Domini system. He'd certainly never bothered to learn it.

The bartender returned with their drinks. The Admiral's was served in a mug, which she seemed to find amusing. Jack thought the brightly coloured glass of orange juice on the coaster in front of him made him look like a child.

He also didn't care. One long gulp later and he was smiling like he'd won a ticket in the Ark lottery. Man, had he missed proper human food. The next time he came to New Terra he would insist on being taken out for a madras.

Providing New Terra still existed tomorrow, that is. Maybe it was just as good he'd turned down the booze, because that thought sure sobered him up.

"So, erm, ma'am." Jack traced lines through the condensation on his glass. "This place is very lovely and all, but why did you bring me here? I'm sure you could call on much more interesting company."

"More interesting? Are you sure?" Blatch scoffed. "Most other humans I speak to have spent just as long a time stuck on this ship as I have, not counting the men and women serving on the planet below. Nobody's got anything even half-interesting to say. You're the man who's seen the galaxy. So, tell me. What's new?"

"What's new? Ha! Trust me, you'd rather not know."

"Humanity won't be confined to just this one world for very long, Mr. Bishop. We already have representatives in extra-terrestrial colonies in dozens of star systems. So if you have insight into anything... shall we say... *concerning* about our neighbours, I'd certainly like to hear it."

Jack took a deep breath. Top-ranking members of the UEC *did* have connections with the Ministry, despite their species not yet belonging to the council. He was almost certain humanity hadn't picked up the emergency broadcast

Tuner sent out, but could one of the aforementioned emissaries have sent word about the attacks from a Krolak or Drygg outpost? Was the Admiral quizzing him on something she already knew?

God, he hated politics.

"A powerful race called the Prymalis are beating the crap out of every major and minor civilisation out there. But instead of uniting everybody in the galaxy like it should, it's dividing us. If we can't fight this threat together, then we'll each die alone. And unfortunately that includes humanity."

"We've only just got here," the Admiral replied, casually sipping her drink. "Surely we're not on their radar."

"Oh, you can bet we are. Have been for a *long* time. They might not see us as much of a threat right now, but sooner or later they'll turn up on your doorstep. And it won't matter how many battlecruisers you have out there – if we're the last species left, they won't be enough."

"Months. It's been *months* since the war with those damn bugs ended. I won't tell you how many people we lost colonising this planet, Mr. Bishop. Too many. Yet it sounds as if you expect us to jump straight into another conflict."

"Better to fight the Prymalis now alongside the mightiest empires in the cosmos than to wait and face them on our own."

"Come on. You just told me the galactic community is more divided than ever. It doesn't sound as if we'd be fighting alongside anyone. And besides, how do you expect humanity to help? From the intelligence we gather, we're one of the least technologically advanced species out there. Our battlecruisers have yet to experience any form of active combat and have been collecting dust in orbit for over a year now. This stays between you and me, but we're hardly the mighty military force you make us out to be."

"Neither are—"

Admiral Blatch raised her hand. Jack fell silent.

"You can't convince me to send my fleets out to fight some celestial threat any more that I could persuade the UEC board members to go along with it. I'm sorry, but let's just leave it at that."

Jack deflated, then returned to his drink. It didn't taste so good anymore.

"Fine. Humanity is exhausted. I get it. If I'd been through what you had, getting slaughtered by roaches and all that, I wouldn't want to rush into another fight either. That wasn't what I came here for, anyway."

He pushed his chair back and rose to his feet.

"You're leaving?" she asked, her glass raised to her lips. "So soon?"

"I'm afraid so. I've got a long flight ahead of me if I'm to make it back to Kapamentis before everything kicks off. The way things have been going lately, this might be the last time we ever meet."

He pulled his data pad out of his pocket – the marines lurking in the corners of the bar stiffened momentarily – and swiped the screen towards the Admiral.

"I've sent you the coordinates for Kapamentis," he said, pocketing the data pad again. "You know, just in case. If we lose this war, everyone's dead anyway. But if we stop the Prymalis and mankind doesn't do its part... well, I hate to think where that leaves us in the galactic community."

He downed the rest of his orange juice and tucked his chair back under the table.

"Thank you for the drink, ma'am. And congratulations on New Terra. It's a planet worth fighting for."

He marched from the room and left a pensive Admiral Blatch to finish her drink alone.

11

THE FATAL DARK

Jack rushed to the bathroom twice in the space of twenty minutes. His stomach was a hessian sack of hot coals one moment, a leaky detergent capsule the next. And the last thing he wanted was to die with a full bladder.

"Still not here yet?" he asked, returning to the cockpit. His hands were almost shaking too much to fasten his spacesuit back together.

"Still not here yet," Tuner replied, casting a pair of LED eyes in Rogan's direction.

"For bolt's sake, I'm not psychic." She shook her head as she consulted Adi's scans. "This is when the Archimandrite said they would strike, and every projective model I ran confirmed as much. Don't blame me, blame the data."

Jack tried chewing the skin around his fingernails but his gloves were in the way. He settled with making a meal of his bottom lip instead.

"And yet..."

The *Adeona* drifted a kilometre outside of Kapamentis's atmosphere, her thrusters off. The surrounding star system was noticeably sparse. And this wasn't just down to the

Prymalis' absence. For all the many hundreds of thousands of species and empires and factions who had surely heard their call for help, very few had actually answered. And even those who did weren't exactly talking to each other.

Half a dozen Ministry frigates held together by nothing more than duct tape and sheer sense of duty skulked on Adi's starboard. Jack trusted a few smaller vessels were patrolling the other side of the planet. Whether Grand Minister Zsal had caved and sent them there or the Ministry's limited local force had taken it upon themselves to defend Kapamentis, he didn't know. He hadn't heard from her since leaving Vekemorte.

The majority of ships present were formed of smaller contingencies from some of the least powerful species in the Ministerium. The Collusect – a hive-mind of skinny, long-necked insectoids no greater than three feet in height – had spared a pair of botanical warships. The feathered peoples of Tukka'shi sent some armoured cruisers and, rather generously, a medical barge. Even a handful of Ubekian Cutworm bombers had shown up. Between the lot of them, they could probably fend off a single Prymalis battleship. Probably.

Something that surprised Jack at first was the flotilla of super-destroyers sent by Negoti. Not any warships from the Ghuk themselves, only their largest corporation – almost a political nation in its own right. Then Rogan reminded him that their largest company headquarters outside of the Ghuk homeworld was on Kapamentis, that destruction of a central galactic hub would be disastrous for Negoti's profits, and suddenly the galaxy made perfect sense again.

"Maybe they heard our broadcast and called off the attack?" Tuner suggested anxiously.

"The Prymalis?" Jack snorted as he settled back into his seat. "They're much too arrogant for that. I reckon it's more likely they weren't ever planning on coming here to begin with."

"I assure you," Rogan said, staring up at him from the hologram table, "my models—"

"I'm not saying you were wrong," Jack said quickly, resisting a groan, "just that maybe the Prymalis made it look like they were planning one thing when really they were doing another. I don't know. None of it makes any difference, does it? Wherever they are, what matters is they aren't here."

"Why don't we call Klik?" Adi asked cheerfully.

"Tried." Jack shook his head. "Still can't reach her. Something's up."

"You don't know that," Rogan replied. "She could still be mid-transit or dealing with another emergency. Though from what I can source on the extranet, the Mansa Empire hasn't suffered any more attacks since Paryx. Yet," she couldn't help adding. "In fact, as of this very moment, there don't appear to be many other invasions taking place at all..."

"Erm, I think there might be a good reason for that," said Tuner, pointing out of the cockpit windows. "Quite a few good reasons, actually..."

Fresh stars blinked into existence against the black backdrop – first one, then a few more, and then hundreds of heart-stopping pinpricks. Legions of Prymalis battleships tore out of subspace, their spiked, fortified hulls shimmering in the dim residual starlight and pulsing with the strange, bioelectric lifeblood that coursed through their purple veins. Jack hadn't seen so many ships in one place since those very same vessels erupted from XO-R15. And in the middle of the cloud of fury and steel was one vessel he truly recognised: the Prymalis flagship. With its round, bulging base and sharp peak, it couldn't be mistaken for anything other than the base of operations in which Jack first encountered the ancient species back on their horrid extroplanet.

The precursor fleet stopped a few hundred thousand kilometres from Kapamentis – roughly the same difference as between the Earth and its Moon. Magnified on the windows of Adi's cockpit, however, their ships could have been within grabbing distance.

"I don't want to say I told you so," Rogan said distract-edly, "but, well…"

"Don't gloat too much," Jack mumbled. "The whole galaxy has never wished you were more wrong."

"I guess we know why the rest of the galaxy got so quiet all of a sudden," Tuner said, slowly retreating behind his computer terminal. "The Prymalis are all here."

"Most of them, certainly. They knew *someone* would put up a fight."

None of the friendly ships moved to engage the lurking threat. Jack guessed the Ministry frigates were instructed to act in a defensive rather than offensive manner. The rest were most likely giving their attendance a second thought.

"Will we, though? I mean, I guess this is it. This is everyone who came to defend Kapamentis. Do you really think this ramshackle lot can put up any sort of fight at all?"

Rogan smiled apologetically.

"Do you actually want me to answer that question?"

"And we really have to go through with this? We can't, know you, accept that we're powerless to stop the Prymalis, fly away to some deserted planet in the arse end of nowhere and live out the rest of our lives in peace?"

"Are you seriously suggesting we let Kapamentis be destroyed?" Tuner's head popped up again. "We can't abandon all of its citizens who can't afford to escape. There are fleshies and automata alike down there. I know we can't win, but..."

"I was only kidding, buddy." Like Rogan, Jack tried to flash a smile, but it just looked as if his stomach cramps had returned. "I don't really want to run. I wouldn't mind being peer-pressured into it, though..."

The bombers belonging to the Ubekian Cutworms ignited their massive hydrogen thrusters. Shortly after, the bark-coated botanical warships booted up their drive cores, too.

"Everyone's getting ready to either fight or flee." Jack grabbed the *Adeona's* accelerator lever with one hand, her flight stick with the other. "We'd better get ready to join them."

"To join them in doing the *first* one," Tuner reminded him.

"Of course," he replied. "Not that there's a lot of good in us charging in there alone..."

Or with anyone else, he thought to himself.

"Ready, Adi?" he asked the ship.

"As I'll ever be," the *Adeona* replied. Her hull trembled as her thrusters roared to life. "Torpedos loaded, cannons primed and ready."

"Hey, guys." Jack glanced over his shoulder. "If this is the end, I just want you all to know what a privilege it's been to spend the last year and a half with you. After everything I've been through – *we've* been through – you're not just friends. You're family. Without you, I'd be...well... let's just say I couldn't have asked for—"

"Shut up, Jack." Rogan enlarged the scans on the holo-gram table, the apertures of her eye-lenses as wide as could be. "What in the name of rusty bolts is happening out there? The map's getting so many pings, I may as well be looking at the fairy lights in Tortaiga Square."

"More Prymalis?" Tuner whimpered.

"No." Jack broke into a grin. "More of *us*."

The arriving ships didn't so much become fresh stars in the dark sky as replace the entire nebulous vista. It looked to the naked eye as if every ship jostled hull to hull, as if they'd formed a physical blockade around the Prymalis fleet, circling them like a Dyson sphere over a star. No organic mind could hope to count the different armadas who burst into the system, let alone the scores of individual ships, but amongst their number were more than a few Jack recognised.

A dozen or more brown Krolak dreadnoughts, distinct in their likeness to an alligator's jaw and overladen with the most vicious weaponry their reptilian warmongers could design, skulked hungrily far on the *Adeona's* port side. Nearby – but not *too* close nearby, Jack noticed – was an Alpha Rhoden fleet consisting of stocky, grey and heavily scarred warships. Not to be outdone by their bitter rivals, the Rhoden had brought almost twice as many ships. It appeared the two empires had each agreed to put aside their dispute for however long it took to bludgeon an even bigger target to a pulp. Provided anyone actually survived this battle, Jack imagined that any respective kill-counts would be compared with *extreme* scrutiny.

The Plillup brought destroyers, which were, as Tuner had once gone to great pains to point out, actually quite impressive. Designed for both submarine and interstellar use, their bright blue destroyers more closely resembled giant, spherical space stations than they did aero- or hydro-dynamic ships. What they lacked in agility they made up for in defence – an aquatic species, and with the interior of their ships entirely filled with water, the Plillup designed monstrously thick hulls that wouldn't buckle under even the most immense pressure. And their fission lasers were known to pack a punch. Jack hoped the Plillup's years of fostering a reputation for peacefulness didn't prevent them from remembering how to use them.

Nestled amongst the botanical warships of the Collusect were more warships that had been grown rather than built. But unlike the Collusect's, which were airtight networks of vines and trunks and other such mega-flora, these were the beloo of the Donto Kabal. Colossal living ships – living in the fleshy, organic sense, unlike the sentient ships who allied with the automata – that harvested energy from stars using their whale-like solar fins, each was capable of harbouring close to a thousand semi-symbiotic pilgrims inside their cetacean cavities as they made the long, dark voyage from one system to another. Not normally a belli-cose people, the Donto Kabal had fitted the few beloo they'd brought with rudimentary skip drives and proton cannons. Honour would have compelled these nomadic communities to fight – it certainly wasn't desire.

Occupying another swathe of the protective shield was an Oortilian flotilla – their battlecruisers, camouflaged to blend in with the floating rocks of Oort Clouds, flanked by hundreds of sleek attack ships barely any larger than personal planet-hoppers. As with the fleet-footed Oortilians themselves, their military strategy relied on lightning-quick manoeuvres rather than brute force.

Elsewhere, the Kwoo Fim – their round, snail-shell destroyers with long, underside rail cannons crawled into position, ready to exact revenge for Yanna Lös. Also present were the Argenta, whose starships sported giant wings that mirrored their species' own impressive wingspans, and two mountainous stone space stations belonging to the Trull-janan – an intelligent species of sedimentary troll that normally kept to itself in the outer systems.

Above the rest, as if presiding over proceedings, were the bony, wraith-like battlecruisers Jack recognised as the Nárva's. Whether they were fresh from defending Veke-morte or had been sent by Grand Minister Zsal from another colony closer by, Jack was pleased to see them, just as he was the gnarly green cruisers sent by the Ghuk, not to be outdone by their own corporation; the Dryggs and their industrial frigates; and the bulbous carriers of the Luethians.

To Jack's even greater surprise was the number of ships in attendance who flew no flag at all. Not only were thousands of mercenaries and well-armed private citizens ready to fight, but so were dozens of notorious pirate clans from outworlds such as Barataria. Even the reviled Black Rock Raiders had shown up. Whether some of the outlaws present were here looking for a pardon or a good fight didn't seem to really matter.

"It worked," Rogan said to Tuner in radiant disbelief. "Your message actually brought everyone together."

All around the star system, thrusters ignited like the starting lights for the universe's most deadly race.

"Come on, guys." Jack shoved the accelerator lever forwards. "Let's help save the galaxy."

12

DIFFERENT/SAME

The Prymalis fleet pressed towards Kapamentis but, with the protective shield of allied ships enveloping them so tightly, were unable to jump to subspace. Without any official word given, the combined forces of the galaxy attacked as one. Casualties were immediately high, beginning with a pirate schooner that enthusiastically tore towards the Prymalis on supercharged plasma thrusters and got eviscerated in an instant. One of the Luethian carriers soon followed.

With thousands of warships and capital ships and attack ships soon blasting one another with lasers and ballistics, it was impossible to calculate who was doing what amongst the frantic fray, let alone which side was winning. Any attempt to tune into the official Ministry comm frequencies was met with a cacophony of alien voices no translator chip could hope to interpret.

Few civilisations present had any prior experience against an empire as powerful as the Prymalis. Fewer still knew what to expect and how to defeat them. The Nárva, the Alpha Rhoden, the Kwoo Fim and Ghuk – these species had engaged a Prymalis battleship before and won, yet only by the skin of their teeth (or beaks). The rest dove in blind.

Skirmishes broke off between Oortilian jet fighters and the spiky, primordial trilobite ships, ducking and swooping around one another like a murmuration of starlings. Battlecruisers fought battlecruisers, bombarding one another with torpedoes and nukes. Some optimistic corvettes even headed straight for the Prymalis mothership, though were quickly cut down by the warships most closely guarding her.

A ship as small as the *Adeona* was soon lost amongst the chaos.

———

THE KROLAK DREADNOUGHTS SLOWLY CLOSED in on the nearest flotilla of the Prymalis fleet. In the cold vacuum of space, the propulsion of their thrusters was almost offset by the steady, pounding recoil of their artillery cannons. Atomics had been fired from an even greater distance, and one of the Prymalis ships now drifted listlessly away from its pack.

"Prepare the Stukka Bombs," snarled Korrga, admiral of the Krolak fleet. She scratched at her scales. The thrill of battle was almost enough to distract her from the bridge's low humidity, but not quite.

The Krolak stationed in the pod beside Korrga's command podium barked orders into his headset. The rest of her bridge was abuzz with the bloodthirsty tension she expected from her crew. Despite signing up for the Krolak navy, she knew many of them would much prefer to be on the ground killing Prymalis with their bare claws. Given the chance, so would she. Millenniums came and went, but it would always remain the Krolak way.

"Stukka Bombs loaded for drop," grunted the Krolak in the pod beside her.

Korrga turned to the pod on the other side of her podium.

"Bring us into position," she snarled.

Her dreadnought ploughed onwards, as did those to either side of her. Whilst her own warship ceased bombarding the Prymalis battlecruisers (though its artillery cannons continued to pepper any light spacecraft that dared come within half a klick of its trajectory), the others assaulted the enemy monoliths with weapons normally put aside for blasting whole asteroids to dust.

A flash from the Prymalis battlecruiser below them. The dreadnought to Korrga's left lurched upwards as something shot up through its underside and exploded out the top of its hull. Pieces of cannons and interior bulkheads splintered outwards. Flames licked hungrily as oxygen and nitrogen fled the breached areas of the ship. The lights in the dreadnought's windows died, came back in shades of red as if the ship were bleeding internally, and then died again in the rear half of the ship. No vessel can live with a hole torn through its belly. A second strike moments later punctured the cockpit, sent an explosive chain reaction through the length of the ship, and sealed its fate.

A number of Krolaks on Korrga's own ship rose from their pods and snapped their jaws in frustration.

"Continue," she growled at them.

The dreadnought fleet trudged on regardless, even as the Prymalis weapon below them began its slow, electrifying charge once more. Their warships were too slow to get out of the line of fire even if they wanted to, but that wasn't the Krolak way. Better to take a hit and keep fighting than turn and run away. Soon, with only a few of its cannons lost to nimble enemy attack ships taking advantage of their exposed flank, the shadow of Korrga's dreadnought fell over its target.

"Now!" she snarled.

The undercarriage of her dreadnought opened; a cloud of small metal orbs was propelled out. They rained down upon the Prymalis battlecruisers, spreading outwards as they fell, adhering themselves to the enemies' hulls like iron spores. A small number were shot down before they reached their targets, and a similar number again detonated as their neighbours blew up, but the vast majority stuck hard against the Prymalis' biomechanical exteriors.

"Payload delivered," the Krolak to Korrga's right said with a smirk on her snout. "Doors closed."

"Elevate and retreat," Korrga said to the operator on her left. "All ships, spread formation."

The Krolak grunted in acknowledgement and relayed the instruction to the rest of the dreadnought fleet. Immediately they began to rise, then retrace their trajectory back towards their original position in the wall of ships protecting Kapamentis.

Their dreadnought took a glancing hit from a Prymalis cannon. Red warning lights flared inside the bridge. Korrga swiped her claws at them dismissively. They weren't dead. One sector lost, if that. Hardly worth wasting a klaxon over.

"Detonation in three..." said the operator, "two... one..."

The metal orbs that clung like barnacles to the hulls of three Prymalis battlecruisers exploded in a triumphant cataclysm – a chain of incendiary dominoes that swept from port to starboard. Their blue nuclear fires burned bright, wrenching the steel frames from the battlecruisers and flooding their insides with the hot plasma of miniature stars. When the fallout cleared, nothing was left of the enemy but sparking shrapnel.

The Krolaks inside the bridge let out guttural roars in celebration. More Prymalis ships altered their course in retaliation. Korrga steeled herself for the long battle ahead.

Three down. Only a hundred times that number to go.

———

THE KWOO FIM fired their railgun, but the Prymalis battleship kept getting closer and closer.

Each electromagnetically-propelled shot hit its target but, no matter how much of the enemy's hull they sheered off, they couldn't seem to destroy it. It was as if the nose of the battlecruiser deflected the worst of the damage away from its vital sectors.

They retreated not out of cowardice, but because their railgun was the most powerful weapon in their destroyer's arsenal. If the Prymalis ship closed the distance, if they couldn't maintain a direct line of sight, there'd be little they could do to stop it from eradicating them instead.

Despite the imminent threat, what constituted a Kwoo Fim command bridge was remarkably calm. Not that many of the operators inside the bridge could see each other to know this, that is. This wasn't because their species was blind – they could 'see' almost as accurately as a human using a highly developed form of echolocation – but rather that all but a few of them were hooked up to virtual reality interfaces.

It's quite normal not to hear what's going on outside your spacecraft. Sound cannot travel through a vacuum, after all. But this poses rather a unique problem for a species that entirely relies on sound for navigation. The Kwoo Fim had no trouble traversing the complicated multi-surface interior of their destroyers, but had zero way of knowing whether they were sailing away from their planet or seconds from crashing into one.

Unable to interpret computer screens for the same reason, the Kwoo Fim used simulations to convert the information received from their ships' radar systems into three-dimensional aural environments. Maps, statistics, messages – those plugged into the system could hear all of it at the equivalent of a glance.

As such, a Kwoo Fim bridge, and indeed any sector of the destroyer that required abstract calculation, resembled less the command room of a UEC battlecruiser and more a damp Internet cafe. Each Kwoo Fim sat in its own shallow pool of water with dozens of electrodes stuck to its tendrils and gelatinous head. Only a few others moved freely around the room to ensure nobody suffered a cerebral haemorrhage or drowned.

Somebody had made a mistake. The small fleet of Kwoo Fim destroyers had separated to target different battleships, each assaulted by warships belonging to other species, rather than stick together as a single force. Following the attack on Yanna Lös, it wasn't believed that the Kwoo Fim military could stand up to a Prymalis ship alone. But now, with an allied Oortilian battlecruiser reduced to a drifting, smouldering wreck, that was exactly the situation this destroyer found itself in, without even its brethren for backup.

And still their railgun failed to penetrate the battleship's shielded bow. More than a few operators' tendrils started to thrash erratically in their VR-pools. Everybody on board knew there wouldn't be time to charge another shot before the enemy passed the railgun and drew adjacent to their left flank.

An order went out to launch their secondary armaments. The simulations updated in real-time to display dozens of missiles streaking out of panels on the side of the destroyer's circular hull. Only a couple managed to break through the Prymalis' shields. A second order went out shortly afterwards instructing everyone to evacuate the ship.

Their electrodes disengaging automatically, all the disoriented Kwoo Fim in the bridge hurriedly climbed out of their pools and headed towards the escape modules. This included those of highest rank – as far as the Kwoo Fim were concerned, if you'd survived enough battles to become the equivalent of a human admiral, you'd earned the right to get off the next doomed ship before anyone else. Seconds later the destroyer rocked as the Prymalis battleship responded with a rocket barrage of its own. This the Kwoo Fim *could* hear, and everybody inside the ship instantly knew that the sectors responsible for life support were gone. There was no saving the vessel now, only what remained of its crew.

Evacuation was a key concern amongst Kwoo Fim shipbuilders, more so with every passing century of peace and prosperity amongst their people. Every sector had an easily-reachable module that could quickly jettison from the main destroyer. One by one the surviving sectors shot away, each tracked with a beacon for retrieval once they were safely in the clear.

Though they remained blind to the battle raging on

around them, those crowded inside the bridge's escape module reduced their panicked warbling. All except the Kwoo Fim responsible for interfacing with the communication and scanner units, who grew more worried still.

The Prymalis weren't blowing up the destroyer anymore. They were targeting the fleeing modules instead.

Even Krolaks weren't heartless enough to do that.

First, those escaping the Gun Deck – the Prymalis eviscerated their module with a single ballistic. Then the next module over – Medical. Following the pattern from starboard to port, the pod housing the bridge operators would surely be next.

The Kwoo Fim monitoring the interface decided not to inform his fellow crew members of this. Better to die in an instant than spend their last few moments dreading it.

But the Prymalis battleship never made the shot.

A beloo belonging to the Donto Kabal – an incorrect observation on the Kwoo Fim's part, as the relationship was far more symbiotic than most species realised – crashed into the side of the enemy ship, knocking it off-course so that the shot intended for the bridge module disappeared into the empty cosmos instead. The Prymalis turrets swivelled and scorched a hole in one of the beloo's rear pectoral fins. The plasma cannons adorning its whale-like back may have been rudimentary, but at point-blank range they broke through the battleship's shields and very nearly the hull opposite, too.

Gutted and inanimate, the battleship drifted away from the giant, melancholic beast. The Kwoo Fim operator let out a warbling cheer that caught its fellow occupants inside the module by surprise.

The beloo's skin briefly shimmered a blue-green shade, a gesture those inside the modules couldn't have understood even had their simulations been able to interpret colour into sound, and swam back towards the conflict.

Only the Donto Kabal could have attempted a direct translation. It meant, to the best of their understanding, the paradoxical similarity between 'one' and 'many' – or, in other words, different and yet the same.

13

OLD "FRIENDS"

The *Adeona* weaved through the fray, more often dodging explosions and debris than enemy attack ships. Whenever Jack spotted a friendly frigate in distress, he brought Adi close enough to help take out the offending party with her rotary cannons. The rest of the time, the crew did everything it could to avoid being noticed – out of all the ships present, they were one of the least suited to all-out war.

In the centre of the maelstrom the Prymalis flagship lay in wait.

"How the hell is anyone supposed to take down that thing?" Jack asked, swooping around the outskirts of the battle. "I mean, just look at it for a second. That's less a mothership and more an armoured asteroid, if you ask me."

"They'd have to get near it first," Tuner replied. "Battleships are swarming every inch of it. It's almost as if that flying base of theirs doesn't have any weapons of its own."

"You're probably right," Rogan said. "The Prymalis have presumably been using it as a base of operations on XO-R15 for centuries. Millennia, maybe. Either way, they likely built it out there, too. Defence is its main objective, not assault."

"Then why did they bring it to a damn dogfight?" Jack shouted, banking hard to the left.

"If it's their primary colony ship," Rogan replied, "then I suspect they intend to land it on Kapamentis. Or what's left of Kapamentis once the rest of the fleet is done with it, at any rate."

"Then I suppose it's of little concern to us, then." Jack swung the *Adeona* back to the right. "Their invasion won't get very far if their whole navy is dead."

"It might if *we're* all dead too," Tuner said quietly.

Jack sent the *Adeona* into a sharp dive as a Prymalis battleship burst out from behind the wreckage of a Negoti super-destroyer. Though Adi was certainly not a small ship by most galactic citizens' standards, she paled in size to the warships attracting most of the enemy's attention. The derelict super-destroyer alone was almost three kilometres long. With Adi's cannons incapable of penetrating a battle-ship's reinforced armour, it was best just to keep out of their way.

Something exploded in their wake. Jack didn't bother to check their rear view and find out what – the important thing was it wasn't them.

They found themselves headed for a Collusect warship. It was engulfed in flames. Blackened vines withered as they retracted into the dying bark. The oxygen that fed the fire got sucked out as gaps appeared across the ship's botanic hull. The glorious flowers sprouting from outside the ship wilted and writhed as their host died. Somewhere out in the wider cosmos the Collusect hive-mind screamed in agony as a hundred souls went silent.

Veering out of a collision course brought no less

haunting a view. Some form of heavy projectile had punctured one of the Plillup destroyers. Small translucent bodies floated out of the open wound in a fountain of crystalline seawater.

Jack lurched the *Adeona* downwards once more, spun her over one-hundred-and-eighty degrees, and continued onwards into comparatively calmer seas.

"There's still no sign of the automata fleet," Tuner said, locking his little metal digits together.

"Don't worry, buddy." Jack bit his lip. "Humanity's a no-show, too. I guess neither of our species sees this as their fight."

"If we don't win," Rogan said darkly, "humanity and the automata might be the only ones *left* to fight. I dare say that war won't last long."

"Distress, distress," a mysterious voice pleaded over Adi's comm system. "We're an infirmary frigate under fire from unidentified attack ships. Our escort has been eliminated. Please assist."

"The Prymalis don't care if that ship's only here to take in the injured." Tuner climbed up on his chair as if afraid the others might not notice him otherwise. "We have to help them!"

"Right you are, Tuner." Jack glanced back at Rogan. "Where's this frigate?"

"NavMap coordinates up now," she quickly replied.

"Tell them we're on our way."

Jack had switched off Adi's thrusters once they were in the clear – as much as anywhere could be considered clear in an active war zone, that is. They were already travelling at a frighteningly quick velocity, and would remain at said velocity indefinitely, given the frictionless vacuum, until an external force was applied... either by them or something else. He rammed the accelerator lever forwards again and sent them racing towards the besieged frigate.

From an outside perspective it was an absurd distance, but the *Adeona* covered it in less than half a minute. Nobody paid them much attention during those thirty tense seconds spent weaving around skirmishes and ducking past ship-wrecked schooners – there were far more tempting targets on offer, most of which lumbered across the battlefield like titanic war elephants. But that changed the moment they paused to take stock of the hapless frigate before them.

"Something's on our tail," Rogan yelled. "It's been following us since the distress call. Bolts alive, it's coming in fast!"

"Goddammit." Jack jerked his flight stick to the right. "Can you track them, Adi? Do you need me to help line up a shot?"

"Negative, Captain." The *Adeona* sounded remarkably cheerful for the situation. "That's hardly an appropriate way to greet old friends."

Jack stared in nauseous trepidation, then hysterical disbelief as a small and sleek private cruiser drew level with them outside the cockpit windows. Rogan and Tuner rushed forwards and crowded around him for a better look.

Four figures waved at them from the *Silver Hart's* chrome cockpit. Sheni Dupont, the human who somehow smuggled himself onto a French Ark during the evacuation of Earth. Gecki, the regenerative reptilian pirate who rescued him after the UEC found out. Xotl, the Xocha starfish exiled from Estroidea who, for contamination reasons, couldn't leave the ship it piloted. And Alan, the unidentified alien species who came with the ship, dribbled and gurgled a lot, and was either the smartest or dumbest creature anyone ever had the fortune to encounter.

"Hey, man." Sheni's voice burst excitedly through the intercom. "Long time no see!"

"What the hell are *you* lot doing here?" Jack replied.

"Where else would we be, right? This is the showdown of the millennium. I mean, Gecki *did* suggest that we raid a few strongholds while everyone else was out here saving the galaxy, but I reminded her that piracy ain't a long-term profession if there's nobody left to pirate, you know?"

"How very noble of you," Rogan said.

"He's being an idiot," Gecki rasped with a roll of her eyes. "We came as soon as we heard Kapamentis was in trouble. We have to live in this galaxy too, you know."

"Picked up your ping while avoiding a Skavian hellfighter," Sheni said. "Yours was the only ship out here we recognised. Well, except for some of the pirates clans', see, but best we steer clear of them, you know? Thought you might fancy some help with that frigate over there."

Jack couldn't help noticing the turrets under the *Silver Hart's* nose and wings.

"I didn't think your stolen ship had guns."

"Stolen is such a dirty word," Gecki hissed. "We liberated it from an undeserving owner and put her to better use. And no, she didn't. Some retired merc had a fighter she wasn't using. We thought its guns needed liberating, too."

Jack laughed.

"Yeah, well, you'd better not 'liberate' anything out here once the smoke clears. Have you got shields on that thing?"

"Nano-reactive superhot air-plasma," Alan said with a gormless smile.

"That's a yes," Xotl gurgled.

"Good." Jack turned back to the frigate. "You're gonna need them."

The infirmary frigate was heavily shielded as well,

which was extra fortunate given it boasted only a few sets of turrets along the top of its long, shovel-nosed bow. All three were spinning wildly and shooting at the Prymalis attack ships peppering its hull with the same powerful ballistic rounds that had shot down the *Adeona* on XO-R15. Though its escort may have been wiped out already, the *Adeona* and the *Silver Hart* weren't the only ones to answer the frigate's distress call. A few Krolak and Drygg attack ships attempted to keep the Prymalis from inflicting any major damage.

"Come on, Jack." Sheni gestured for Xotl to pilot the ship forwards. "We can't let these aliens take all the credit. The ship with the fewest kills gets the rounds in, yeah?"

"That would involve paying for something," Jack scoffed. "As if you'd actually—"

"Sounds good," Adi replied enthusiastically, pushing her thrusters to full power.

Jack struggled to regain some semblance of control before they re-entered an active war zone. He didn't know what Adi was so excited about. She couldn't even drink.

The *Adeona* had received plenty of upgrades over the years, but as a repurposed mining vessel she hadn't the streamlined frame (not to mention super-expensive) drive core of the *Silver Hart*, which slipped through the dark expanse like a crossbow arrow launched into the night. Still, Adi closed the distance in almost no time at all and, unlike Sheni and Gecki's ship, she not only had guns – she knew how to use them.

"Take as much evasive action as you need, Jack," she said menacingly. "You won't throw off my aim."

"I'm not sure I like how much you're enjoying this," Jack mumbled under his breath.

From a glance he could make out a little short of a dozen Prymalis attack ships. They intermittently shot at the frigate and the Krolak and Drygg ships defending it, flitting and swerving around in erratic orbits. Jack didn't know where to start.

"Bottom left," Adi said as if reading his thoughts. She highlighted the enemy ship on her window. "It's a straggler."

Jack sent the *Adeona* down to the left; the *Silver Hart* had already banked towards the fiercer fray towards the right. He hoped they were all right. They may have been greedy, backstabbing pirates, but they were still putting their lives at risk while many others decided to hide. Fortunately, the Krolaks were fighting on that side of the frigate too.

The hospital ship's shields shimmered a dark blue where each projectile hit. Jack noticed a delayed crackle – if the frigate wasn't given a break to recharge its shields soon, it'd lose them completely.

Adi opened fire on the Prymalis attack ship as soon as she was in range. Jack kept her on a pursuit course – as far as he could tell, the Prymalis didn't have rear-facing guns. It tried to spin around in a sharp circle, but Adi's rounds tore through it before the manoeuvre could be completed. The attack ship exploded and bashed inertly against the frigate's hull.

Even Jack couldn't help letting out a little cheer.

A second attack ship screeched out from underneath the frigate before his mouth could finish turning up at the corners. Jack banked hard to the side as a barrage of projectiles shot past them – one skimmed their own shields and sent a harrowing shiver through Adi's hull.

"You got it, Adi?" he screamed.

"Oh, I've got it…"

The *Adeona's* rotary cannons kept track of the attack ship as they spiralled around in parallel, neither gaining on the other. Jack used her air thrusters to perform a quick turn, changing their trajectory so they were suddenly headed straight for the enemy. He swore as the Prymalis ship mirrored his movements, forcing him into another rolling dive.

Despite his erratic flying, Adi didn't seem the least bit fazed. She let loose with both of her turrets, spraying in a helix pattern as they spun away from the attack ship. She even cut out each weapon in time with her roll to avoid accidentally hitting the frigate instead. The attack ship couldn't strafe out of the way of her barrage quickly enough. The spines jutting out from its rear got clipped, and then a more precisely targeted round from Adi punctured its core and left it floating lifelessly away.

"Consider this payback for downing me on that cruddy planet," Adi gleefully boasted, "you bunch of craggy old space-trash."

Jack didn't wait for a third attack ship to introduce itself, boosting them higher and higher (from their perspective, at least) until they could get a better, safer look at the skirmish. Thankfully, nothing angry followed. Both the Krolaks and the Dryggs had lost a fighter each – well, Jack could identify two mangled wrecks he assumed belonged to friendlies, though he supposed countless more could have been destroyed entirely – but taken out three times as many Prymalis attack ships in return. Only a handful remained, though it was doubtful for very long.

"Erm, guys?" He addressed the question to Rogan and Tuner but kept his eyes on the battle ahead. "Does anyone see the *Silver Hart* anywhere?"

"Oh, bolts." Tuner cradled his cassette-shaped head in his hands as Jack slowly edged the *Adeona* back towards the fight. "I should have told them that ship of theirs wasn't built for combat…"

"Did you see that, Jack?" Sheni's voice boomed over comms as the *Silver Hart* swept out from behind the other side of the frigate. "We got one! You'd better get your wallet ready, man, coz—"

The infirmary frigate exploded in an orb of blinding white fire. Jack shielded his eyes and wrestled with the flight stick as Adi rocked backwards from the force of the blast. Tuner fell off the back of his chair despite the *Adeona's* artificial gravity systems. Alarms bleated in the cockpit automatically. The ship quickly shut them off.

"I'm fine," Adi said. "Just a gyroscopic error. Nothing to worry about."

"What the hell just happened?" Jack asked, shaking his head clear.

The flaming remains of the frigate pelted outwards in every direction like the fizzling strands of a firework. Every inch of the ship had been torn apart and twisted by the intense heat. Nothing inside could have survived such a blast; indeed, anything that wasn't a hull, floor or bulkhead had been scorched beyond recognition. One of the Drygg attack ships protecting the vessel limped away from the scene with black smoke billowing from its thrusters.

"Sheni? Gecki?" Jack shouted into comms. "Are you still there? Do any of you read me?"

"Yeah, yeah, we hear you, man. Maybe keep your voice down, all right? My head's still ringing."

The *Silver Hart* had been propelled outwards along with half the frigate and only now got her thrusters back online. Xotl ceased her spinning and brought the ship to an abrupt stop about a klick from where the Kerulian armada was advancing. Her chrome shell was in dire need of new paintwork.

A Prymalis battleship stalked above the ruins. The enormous cannon on its "deck" (from the *Adeona's* perspective, it flew upside-down) still glowed from the shot that obliterated the infirmary ship. The battleship fired a second shot from a smaller turret and the wounded Drygg fighter exploded in a shower of sparks.

"Get the hell out of here," Jack screamed to the crew of the *Silver Hart*. "We can't take on something that massive!"

"You think we don't know that?" Gecki replied. "Why are *you* still here, idiots?"

Jack rammed the accelerator lever forwards. Nothing happened.

"Erm, Adi? What's going on?"

"Just recalibrating my gimbals," the ship replied apologetically. "Something must have got knocked loose in the explosion..."

"We're quite fine with flying in any direction, Adi," Rogan snapped. "Because the only wrong direction is *staying right here!*"

With every other ship having fled the wreckage, the same turrets that killed the Drygg now swivelled to face the *Adeona*.

Jack swallowed hard.

"Adi... just move!"

"I'm trying!"

"Oh no," Tuner said, covering his head with his hands.

Suddenly, the Prymalis ship was subjected to hundreds of explosive missiles. The sustained force broke through its shields and cracked the battleship in half. Jack could scarcely believe his eyes as he watched it detonate from stern to bow.

"Aha!" Tuner jumped on top of his computer terminal. "I *knew* we wouldn't sit this one out!"

The entire automata fleet skipped into the system –

hundreds of sentient warships and destroyers and gunships piloted by the free citizens of Detri. Jack even spotted the flying gothic cathedral that once belonged to the Archimandrite amongst their number, this time surely captained by the LX-14s with whom he sought to commit genocide.

"Glad to see you're keeping out of trouble," Tork's voice said over comms. "We thought the fleshies could use a hand, given it seems they're incapable of doing most things without us."

"Took you long enough to show up," Jack gasped, catching his breath as the automata fleet swallowed the *Adeona*.

"It's a long trip, and we made a slight detour. We brought Max's device from Kondath."

"Why?" Rogan asked. "The bomb's no use outside of an atmosphere. And surely you don't expect us to wait until after they destroy Kapamentis."

"I'll explain later," the cranky automata replied. "First we must keep the tide from turning in the enemy's favour. It appears the Prymalis have brought some reinforcements of their own."

True enough, fresh Prymalis battleships had skipped into the system from various subspace highways and were now attacking the tired allied fleets from behind. Whoever ruled inside that giant Prymalis flagship of theirs must have ordered every last battlecruiser attacking a nearby colony to come bolster their ranks instead.

The automata fleet supercharged its thrusters just as Adi finally got her gyroscopes under control.

"For Detri, friends," Tork declared. "Let's show everyone who the real superpower in this galaxy is."

14

A BIGGER TRIGGER

It seemed to Jack, as he ducked and dodged around the battlefield trying to avoid one-on-one conflict, that as many derelict ships occupied the territory above Kapamentis as active ones. Despite the heavy casualties, or perhaps because of them, it still wasn't possible to tell which side was winning. His gut told him the Prymalis weren't losing, though.

The automata fleet ploughed into the conflict – sometimes literally, in the case of a few old planet-cracker ships. Jack didn't know which cruiser Tork was in, or if any of his friends like Kansas had joined the fight along with him. Perhaps it was better that way. The fight against the Prymalis felt personal enough without worrying about the fate of specific ships.

God, he didn't like how cold that sounded.

The *Adeona* slingshotted past a Plillup destroyer, firing off a spurt of rounds at an enemy fighter on the tail of a raider schooner. It blew up, but Adi was long gone before the schooner could think to thank them.

A formation of private ships tore through the centre of

the battle, submitting one of the Prymalis battleships to a wide variety of explosive weaponry – disintegrators, incinerators, miniature nukes. They were certainly a team of some kind, though each model of ship was unique and Jack spotted no signifiers painted onto their hulls. Mercenaries, he supposed.

A Ghuk frigate slipped above one of the larger Prymalis vessels while it was distracted by a squadron of small Oortilian attack ships. As many as a hundred industrial hatches swung open along its underside and expelled jets of green acid from vats stored in its belly. The corrosive liquid passed undetected through the Prymalis shields and burned through first the Rakletts' ramshackle armour plating and then the biomechanical blackness of its fuselage. The battleship's turrets continued to fire at the Oortilians even as the rest of it melted apart.

Jack swerved to avoid the debris falling off it, then did a double-take. A humongous eyeball stared at him through the cockpit window. Pulling away revealed the eye to belong to a beloo. It was dead, as no doubt were its nomadic Donto Kabal occupants. Frozen blood seeped through a deep gash across its throat. A hole had been burned through one of its pectoral fins, too.

"What in the galaxy is that?" Tuner asked.

"A dead space-whale," Jack sighed.

"Not the beloo, you idiot. *That!*"

A flat, disc-shaped spaceship swam through the various firefights like a stingray. Scatterings of EMPs the size of footballs shot out of its rear every few seconds like flares. The Prymalis attack ship chasing it caught one in its spikes and froze in a cloud of electrostatic bolts.

"I think that's a Bursaag bissön," Rogan said, taken aback. "They're usually only used for ceremonial purposes.

I guess Max's people want everyone to know they aren't quite so insular after all."

"Hey, we'll take all the help we can get." Jack opened the private comm channel they'd established with the automata fleet. "Speaking of which... Tork, you still out there?"

"Of course I'm still out here," the cantankerous robot replied. "Where else would I be?"

"Fancy telling us why the hell you brought a biological weapon designed for inner atmospheric deployment to a war set inside a vacuum?"

"He has a point, Tork." Rogan studied an ever-evolving holo-map of the war zone. "Max's bomb was a stroke of genius, if you can describe the systematic extermination of an entire species in such a way. But it needed to be set off on XO-R15. I'm afraid that ship has sailed."

"Thousands of ships, actually," Tuner added, peering anxiously at all the Prymalis battlecruisers on Rogan's diorama.

"Just because you three bolt-buckets gave up on that idea didn't mean we did," Tork replied. He sounded about ready to blow a gasket. "Doon and Kruzer relayed everything A.M.I. discovered back to me. Given all the advantages these ancients have over us, we couldn't let any possible edge of our own go to waste."

Jack guided the *Adeona* as far out from the fighting as possible without looking as if they were retreating. Unlike the rest of his crew, he couldn't think strategy and pilot the ship at the same time.

"Of course, by all means bring the bomb with you. Better out here than stuck on Kondath, I guess. I was just hoping you had some rhyme or reason for doing it, that's all. Like, oh, I don't know... a plan!"

Tork hissed and clanked.

"What is it about fleshies that make some of you so impatient?" he asked. "Short lifespans, I suppose? I was just getting to that part!"

"Well, can you get to it a little faster? Because I don't know if you've noticed the battle going on around us, but some of us might have very short lifespans indeed!"

"Yes, yes, fair enough. Bolts alive... Where was I? Right. A.M.I. continued to research the device after you lot left, see? Mostly for its own curiosity, if you ask me, but it inspired the AI to develop a few ingenious solutions of its own. Solutions that might render Max's bomb a little more effective than you think."

Jack shivered at the use of the word *solutions* to describe weapons of mass destruction. It reduced whoever was on the receiving end to nothing more than a client's problem that needed permanently "solving". But he supposed it was daft to expect anything else from an artificially intelligent arms dealer.

"Yes?" Rogan asked. "And they are?"

"Slow-impact drills," Tork replied. "Well, that's how A.M.I. described them after nobody could understand its technical gibberish. Using miniature thrusters to slip through shields undetected, they latch onto a ship's hull and burrow inside. But they don't leave an entry point," he hurriedly added. "Only the drill breaks through – the thruster unit remains latched onto the outside like a plug. Then, once a tunnel is bored, the payload is delivered."

"The fleets here have brought all manner of different weapons with them," Tuner said. "I'm not sure a fancy drill is going to be what turns the tide of this battle in our favour. No offence."

"The drill isn't the important bit – the payload is! It's the same toxin as that inside of Max's bomb!"

For a moment, everyone inside the *Adeona's* cockpit was too stunned to speak.

"A.M.I. synthesised the neurotoxin?" Rogan shook her head. "How *did* it get inside without setting it off? *Did* it set it off?"

"More importantly," Jack added, "if we can mass-produce biological weapons specifically targeting Prymalis DNA, why the hell aren't we already using them?"

"Well, not exactly." Tork's pistons wheezed. "The drills don't actually contain the same payload, but they *can* deliver it. It's an... it's a... How did that blasted AI put it... Ah yes, it's a replicator. Each drill is designed to replicate and multiply whatever chemical compound is put into it. Hopefully Max's neurotoxin, in this case."

Jack shut his eyes and groaned.

"And how are we supposed to get Max's bioweapon out of the bomb and into these drills, huh? We're in bloody space, if you hadn't noticed, and the bomb needs to go off inside an atmosphere."

"Ah, well, that's the simple bit. We have an atmosphere in which to detonate it. And the Prymalis battleships are protecting it so closely, they'll almost certainly be caught in the blast zone."

"The flagship," Jack said. "Their flying base of operations. The most inaccessible ship in their entire fleet."

"A.M.I. rigged Max's bomb up to a cluster of atomic warheads," Tork continued. "If we can set it to blow inside their flagship's core, the resulting explosion will not only take out the Prymalis leadership but also carry whatever air the ancients breathe – plus the payload that infects it – to the battleships tasked with protecting them."

"And then the drills will replicate and dispense the payload inside *their* hulls, killing the rest," Tuner said. "Sort of like a chain reaction. Are you sure the toxin will carry far enough, though? What if it, erm, dissipates too much?"

"According to Doon and Kruzer, it shouldn't matter. Space is a vacuum, discounting radiation, cosmic rays and the odd neutrino. Even if a drill only picks up a molecule or two of Max's toxin, that'll be enough to trigger its replication sequence. That's what A.M.I. told them, anyway."

The channel fell silent. Jack ran his hands down his face.

"I mean, it makes sense in theory... right?"

"Say we *do* get Max's bomb inside the Prymalis flagship and set it off, and say the resulting explosion *does* carry the neurotoxin to all the other battleships in their fleet." Rogan leaned across the hologram table, her face stern. "What's to say the payload will actually reach the Prymalis inside? It might kill a few, sure, but all the crew needs to do is block off that section of the ship and they're safe. Ships are built with those sorts of breaches in mind!"

"We may have an answer for that," an uninvited party interrupted over the comm system.

"Who's that?" Rogan asked, standing bolt-upright. "Have you been listening in to this whole conversation?"

"Of course we have," the mysterious, raspy voice answered. "Near enough every species in the galaxy is out here launching gods know what – do you really think we *wouldn't* check in on what they're all saying? This is Reevan, Senior Advisor for the Ghuk armada. Cast your eyes over the schematics I just sent you."

Rogan beamed the file in question above the hologram table. Jack handed over control to Adi and joined her. It was a cutaway drawing of a Prymalis battleship – he recognised the shape from the hundreds still fighting outside the cockpit windows.

"We pieced together what we could from the wreckage above Yanna Lös," Reevan explained. "Nárva researchers on Vekemorte assisted, too. It's far from a perfect layout, but check out the section marked *0332*."

Rogan highlighted the section of ship in question.

"What's so special about it?" she asked.

"We can't be certain, but we believe this is the compartment responsible for each ship's core life support systems. Not every vessel will have the same design, of course..."

"But even if they blocked that compartment off," Tuner said excitedly, "their atmospheric generators would carry Max's toxin around the rest of the ship!"

"Surely they'll have backups," Rogan said.

"Possibly," Reevan replied. "We haven't yet identified which compartments those systems would be located in, but we certainly can't afford to dismiss the idea. Of course, by the time they realise their air is toxic, it may be too late for them to make the switch."

"Or enough of their crew will die that they'll be forced to retreat," Jack suggested. "Either way, it's one step closer to a win."

"This is the genocide of a whole species we're talking about," Rogan said, her voice barely rising above a whisper. "It's not something we should discuss lightly."

"I don't like the idea any more than you do," Jack replied, "but one species eradicated to save hundreds of thousands? If you ask me, there's no discussion to be had."

"It was always going to end this way," Tuner said nervously. "We're already trying to kill them all with rockets and ballistics, aren't we? Now it's just a case of deciding how quickly we pull the trigger."

"And how many good people die before we do," Jack added sternly.

Rogan sighed and nodded.

"Tork, did you get all that? Can the automata fleet ensure those drills target the right compartments on the Prymalis ships?"

"You can bet your bolts we can," the grumpy robot replied. "I'll pass the order down the line. Don't stop trying to blow the ugly brutes up, though."

"Good luck," Reevan said, also cutting comms.

Jack, Rogan and Tuner turned from the hologram table and faced the incomprehensible fracas out beyond the nose of the *Adeona*.

"So I guess this is it," Jack said. "We have a plan. Now all we need to do is figure out how to get that bomb of Max's onto the most heavily defended mothership in the galaxy."

15

OUT OF THEIR DEPTH

The crew of the *Adeona* searched for the *Alnitak*. They had a lock on its beacon, but the landscape was constantly changing, and every time they thought they were close another enemy battleship would turn towards them and they'd be forced to find a safer route around.

It seemed the combined strength of the galaxy wasn't enough. Perhaps they'd waited too long; perhaps each species should have sent more ships instead of holding some back to defend their homeworlds, space stations and colonies. The fleets on both sides were visibly depleted, but the Prymalis still had hundreds of ships left, and their flagship still made its slow, relentless advance towards Kapamentis.

The Argenta were all gone. Jack hadn't seen anything from the Kwoo Fim in a while. Even the Krolaks, who were known to wade enthusiastically into battle no matter the odds, were down to fewer than half the destroyers they arrived with.

And the automata, despite being late to the party, had already suffered considerable losses.

"Prymalis attack ship, on our right," Rogan yelled.

Jack kept the *Adeona* on course for the *Alnitak*; Adi swivelled her rotary cannons and let rip before the attack ship could turn to engage them. It exploded half a second before they disappeared behind an Oortilian battlecruiser.

"We've got a visual on you, Tork," Tuner said, pointing at a giant grey frigate lurking on the edge of the conflict. "Are you ready for us?"

"Head to Hangar 18," Tork replied over comms. "Doon and Kruzer are transporting Max's device down there now."

"Oh God," Jack sighed. "I forgot how heavy that thing is."

He handed controls back to the *Adeona*, who guided them towards the appropriate set of blast doors. More Prymalis attack ships peppered the *Alnitak's* flank but nothing in their arsenal – nor the occasional missile from neighbouring battleships – could penetrate its shields. The frigate's massive artillery cannons made short work of them, swatting them as if they were flies bothering a cumbersome desert beast.

The doors to Hangar 18 rumbled shut as soon as Adi passed through them. Jack wondered how they could be opened so casually, then remembered that everybody on board the *Alnitak* – save for himself, now – was an automata. Most didn't require an atmosphere to function and it cut down on the risk of electrical fires. No oxygen, no fuel for the flames. He was glad he already had his helmet on.

Down the stairs to the cargo bay he ran, following Rogan and Tuner, discovering the *Adeona's* loading ramp already open and a bunch of fretful automata crowding around the bottom. He pushed through them and searched the hangar for their secret weapon.

"Where's Doon?" he asked Rogan. "Where's Kruzer? Aren't they supposed to be here with the bomb by now?"

"Let's try not to panic," Tuner said. "We're in an even bigger and more armoured ship than we were before. And even if something happens, the neurotoxin in Max's device can't hurt you, remember?"

"The nukes strapped to it might," Jack snapped. He craned his neck to see above the automata hurriedly refuelling sentient fighter jets nearby. "And it's getting closer to us with every passing second!"

"It's supposed to be, at any rate." Rogan crossed her arms. "This *is* concerning. It's not like Tork to be so—"

"There they are!" Tuner pointed at the other end of the hangar. "Oh. Well, there *somebody* is, at least."

Two security bots marched towards them. Every other automata was quick to get out of their way, even those tending to the ships. Whether they were the same units as those who once escorted them to A.M.I.'s workshop on Kondath or simply identical models, Jack didn't dare presume.

"Come with us," the robot to the right droned.

"Why? What's going on?" Jack asked. "The bomb is supposed to be here already."

"A proton torpedo from a Prymalis battleship overloaded this ship's shields one minute and thirteen seconds ago. This produced a mild electromagnetic pulse. Regrettably, the cargo elevators for this sector no longer function. The package has been rerouted to Hangar 22 instead."

"Then we'll take the *Adeona*," said Rogan, pulling the others back to the ship. "It'll be quicker."

"Negative," the other robot stated. "The *Adeona* is to go on ahead. You three will be briefed en route while the package is loaded. Please comply. Time is finite."

"Sure, I guess." Jack shrugged uneasily. "If these are Tork's orders…"

"This way," both security bots said in unison. They turned and marched towards a transit corridor like a pair of highly-weaponised cranes.

"See you in a few minutes," Rogan said to the *Adeona* as she took off for the hangar doors again.

They were escorted through the bowels of the old frigate. Jack jumped as every impact on the goliath's shields trembled through her bulkheads and shook dust from the pipes running overhead. The sooner he could get off the *Alnitak* and back on board the *Adeona*, the better.

An old flying automata, carried by a set of whirring propellors, buzzed down the corridor and came to a wobbling stop in the middle of the two security bots. It reversed, struggling to maintain pace with them, and the screen that dominated its entire front switched on.

"My apologies for the disruption," said Tork. The picture showed him scuttling across the *Alnitak's* bridge. "This ship was built strong enough to lug planetary chunks across the galaxy, but those blasted ancients are hitting us with missiles I've never seen before. I think they'd use their solar beams to glass us if their own battleships weren't in the way."

"All the more reason we need to get Max's bomb and be on our way," Rogan replied.

"Agreed. Kruzer assures me that they're loading it onto Adi this very minute, thank the Great Engineer. Delicate business. I do hope you're being careful out there. She's covered in dents."

"Nothing that won't buff out," Jack said tersely.

"Your guards said you needed to brief us," Tuner said,

hopping up and down to make sure he was caught in the frame of the flying automata's camera.

"Yes, yes. Of course. What did that insect say... Oh, yes. Now, we're confident that A.M.I.'s modifications to Max's bomb will destroy the Prymalis flagship – or rather, confident that it'll kill every Prymalis housed inside. But nobody – yourselves excluded, of course – had set eyes on the flagship before this firefight. We've no way of truly knowing how robust its exterior hull might be."

"Are you telling us there's no guarantee the neurotoxin will reach the other battleships?" Rogan asked. "Because if so, Max's contribution to this super-weapon is rather redundant! Any large explosive would do."

The *Alnitak* shook from another enemy bombardment. Jack shivered. Those shields wouldn't hold forever, and a long corridor remained ahead of them.

"Exactly," Tork continued, "and we can't have that. That Ghuk – Reevan was its name, right? – tells me they now have a rudimentary scan of the flagship. The Negoti Corporation used their planet-cracker scanners, apparently. Hard to pinpoint an exact layout, though – shifted about like an eel in a rainstorm, they said – but one of the few sectors they *could* identify was some form of quantum core. Could be powering the thing, could be doing something else entirely. But it's certainly something the Prymalis won't want going *boom*."

"A reactor for a ship that size, coupled with A.M.I.'s nuke cluster?" Tuner let out an electronic whistle. "That'll be one big kablooey."

"Enough to send Max's payload across the battlefield?" Jack asked.

"You bet your bolts it will be," Tuner replied. "Even

without the toxin, an explosion like that could take out half the enemy battleships!"

"We'll need to make sure everyone on our side knows to get clear before it goes off," Rogan said. "I'm not comfortable sacrificing anyone, even if it means ending the Prymalis sooner."

"The message will be relayed," Tork assured her. "There are open channels. I'm not sure how many operators will listen to an old bolt-bucket like me, but I'll do my best."

"And the drills?" Jack asked.

"Holding off for now," Tork wheezed. "We planted a few, though half of those Prymalis battleships have since been destroyed by the Alpha Rhoden. No use in wasting them – we'll deploy the rest once you're inside that flagship. Whatever you do, just make sure that bomb gets triggered inside the—"

The *Alnitak* bucked violently as the Prymalis missiles finally broke through her shields. The wall of the transit corridor ruptured inwards. Up became down as the floor and ceiling gave way.

A torrent of coolant rushed in and knocked Jack off his feet.

Everything went black.

———

A SCORE of golden knives stabbed out of subspace. They lingered on the edge of the battle as if taking in the scene before them – a tangle of shattered ships and frozen bodies above a black planet distinguishable only by its endless shroud of city lights.

Grand Minister Philo Na Ji marched to the observation

window of the bridge, sucked in a lungful of hot, dry and heavily recycled air, and shook his head mournfully.

"So much loss already," he sighed. "Shame the gods. We should have come sooner."

"If it weren't for the colonies seeking revenge for Paryx," the general in charge of the armada replied, "we wouldn't have come at all. This isn't our fight, Philo Na Ji."

"It's everyone's fight," the Grand Minister grumbled. His fleshy eyebrow tendrils quivered. "Either follow your orders, General, or you can step aside for someone who will."

"As you wish, *acting leader*." The spiteful general turned to the rest of the bridge. "Everybody to your stations. Prepare to engage hostiles and provide support for our—" he glanced back at Philo Na Ji with a distasteful look on his face "—*allies*."

The Grand Minister – he hoped, should they survive this war, that the title might return to meaning something – studied the various Mansa operating the battlecruiser. How many of them hated him for the changes he'd made to their empire's culture in only the past few days? How many present felt any duty at all to defend the wider galaxy? He couldn't know – would never know, most likely, given the stigma surrounding social insubordination. Even the general had crossed a line, forgetting, perhaps, that to criticise his leader was to criticise the empire itself. Or maybe the man was owed more credit than Philo gave him, predicting, quite correctly, that such archaic nonsense would be amongst the next set of traditions to go.

One thing Philo Na Ji did know, however, was that not a single other soul on board knew what he'd told the crew of the *Adeona* back in Salyn One, that the ship they worked to pilot – with its black, twisted, semi-organic metal on the inside and golden plates where everyone else could see –

was built around retro-engineered Prymalis technology. That coming to the aid of their fellow species was not some favour graciously granted by a superior empire, but a responsibility they'd had coming for over a thousand years.

Well, *one* other person on board knew the truth. And it was at that moment she came striding onto the bridge beside him.

"By the gods," Klik gasped, her mandibles flaring. "It's a massacre out there. How is anyone still alive?"

One of the Mansa operatives closest to them scowled at the sound of Klik's voice, caught the disapproving eye of the Grand Minister, and hurriedly returned one hundred percent of her attention to the terminal in front of her.

"The *Adeona*! They'll have been out here since the start!"

Klik scrambled to pull her data pad out of the pouch on her sleeveless spacesuit.

"Jack?" she shouted into it. "Rogan, Tuner are you there? Do any of you read me?"

No reply. She shook her data pad frantically.

"Jack?"

"JACK?"

He came to and, blinking sluggishly, discovered he was floating in a black void. Was he drifting helplessly through space again? Everything sure looked dark enough. But no stars. No sign of any derelict ships around him, either.

"Please, somebody answer me! I need to know you're okay!"

"Klik?" Jack mumbled into his comms unit. "Is that you?"

"Jack! Thank the gods. Where are you?"

"Don't know." His words sounded dry and slurred inside his helmet. "Been trying to reach you for ages."

"I've been in sub—" Jack imagined Klik shaking her head in frustration. "It doesn't matter! Are you okay? Where's everybody else?"

"I was on the *Alnitak*. An automata ship. It got hit. Adi was in a different hangar when it happened. Rogan, Tuner... I'm not sure what happened to them."

"Okay... okay... can you at least tell me where *you* are?"

"Hold on."

He switched on the flashlight on his suit and discovered that rather than be ejected from the ship, he'd been submerged in the coolant fluid that flooded out of the breach in the wall. In his struggle to right himself, he knocked loose a broken valve floating beside him. Escaping bubbles floated up towards the ceiling, which at least meant the ship's artificial gravity generator was still operational.

"I appear to be underwater."

"How in the galaxy did you manage that? Never mind. Find a way out of there. I'll keep trying to reach the others."

Klik disappeared. Jack's blood pounded in his ears. Maybe it was just the flashlight reflecting off his visor, but it looked like a hairline crack lurked in the bottom right corner of his helmet.

Well, he was underwater and gravity was working. His best chance at reaching somewhere dry was by heading up.

A more concentrated study of his surroundings suggested he was no longer inside the narrow transit corridor between hangars. The beam of his flashlight only just reached the walls to either side of him and the floor, presuming everything wasn't upside down, was an impossible black chasm beneath his dangling feet. The coolant must have washed him away in a current. Perhaps he'd been sucked back inside the coolant vats while knocked out.

It was a long time since he last went swimming, and his spacesuit, while comfortable, wasn't the ideal outfit for navigating an environment with *increased* pressure. He kicked upwards, hands outstretched to the ceiling, and soon grew frustrated by his lack of progress. Then he remembered the miniature air thrusters Tuner had installed in his gloves and boots. Activating them, he suddenly found himself propelled towards the metal bulkhead almost fast enough to finish cracking his helmet wide open.

Christ alive. People were dying out there trying to stop the Prymalis from razing Kapamentis to the ground. He didn't have time for this.

Keep calm, he told himself. *You could be losing oxygen. And if you panic and get lost down here, you won't be any good to anyone. You got in here somehow – figure a way back out.*

Jack used a girder to pull himself along the ceiling, ignorant of whether he was headed further towards Hangar 18 or 22 or God knows where else. Patience, not panic. If he was methodical in his approach, he'd find a way out. The coolant had flooded into the transit corridor – he remembered that much before blacking out. That meant *he* should be able to get back in there, too.

There. He caught it as his flashlight swept hopelessly from one side of the vat to the other. A hole not in the ceiling, but the wall. Then, noticing the metal staircase leading up to it from the shadowy depths, Jack realised it wasn't the jagged, buckled breach he saw earlier but an open doorway.

Faced with that or braving the swallowing darkness below him, he decided to take his chances with the route marked *Exit*, even if it was spelt out in alien runes.

He used his air thrusters to gently guide himself over,

then paused in the doorway long enough to understand that he wasn't in the vat from which the coolant escaped but some kind of flooded storage warehouse. As his eyes adjusted to the shadows and torch-light, he made out the skeletal frames of empty shelves looming like whale bones picked clean on the ocean floor.

The corridor on the other side of the door wasn't much more welcoming, but Jack could at least see both walls plus the floor and ceiling at once. It wasn't the transit corridor, however. Goddammit. He must have been washed further from the accident than he thought.

"Come on, Jack," he said to himself. "This corridor only goes two ways. Just pick one and be done with it."

"This is the UECS *Invincible* to Jack Bishop," a distinctly human voice suddenly asked over his open comm channel. "Jack Bishop, do you read?"

"Yes? Sorry, who is this?"

"One moment, please."

"Oh, yes. Sure. I'll hold." Jack frustratedly pulled himself along the submerged, derelict corridor. "Don't mind me, I've got all the time in the bloody world."

"Jack," Admiral Blatch said casually, taking over the line from her operator. "I'm surprised you're still alive."

"Not for much longer, I'm sure. I'm sorry, Admiral. This really isn't the best time."

"I can see that. Are galactic wars usually this disastrous?"

"You're here?" Jack banged into an exposed electrical box in his surprise. "The UEC is *here*? Above *Kapamentis*?"

"I'm beginning to wish we weren't. The board took some convincing and they'd only spare three cruisers, but yes, we're here to help however we can. Sorry we almost missed the party."

"Hey, better late than never. We haven't even brought out the cake yet."

God, he hoped the bomb hadn't detonated when the *Alnitak* got hit. It wasn't the frigate he worried for, nor even their super-weapon, but Adi. According to Tork, the neurotoxin-nuke hybrid had already been brought inside her cargo bay when the attack happened.

But if it *had* gone off, wouldn't he have been incinerated too? Or was a million gallons of coolant enough to shield him from the immediate blast? Surely not.

There was no use in speculating. He needed to get out of the water before he ran out of oxygen or the Prymalis finished the job with another missile.

"Get me up to speed, Mr. Bishop. Is there a coordinated strategy in place I should know of?"

He debated whether to fill her in on the fine details, then decided against it. There were too many components to explain and too little time, especially if Max's bomb was no longer an option.

"Well, nobody's really talking to each other, but everyone's launching everything they've got at the bastards in the middle. Welcome to the galaxy, Admiral – that's about as complicated as any plan gets."

"Good grief, Jack." Blatch sounded genuinely pissed off. "No wonder your side isn't winning!"

"*Our* side, Admiral. Look, the Prymalis are wiping out armadas far more advanced than anything humanity has. You might want to provide support from a distance."

"I think I know how best to captain my own fleet, Mr. Bishop."

"And my crew and I are the only people who've ever met the Prymalis and lived," he reminded her. "The UEC doesn't have shield tech yet, does it? A couple of blasts from their cannons and you're toast."

"Hmm. You take care of your ship, Jack, and I'll take care of mine. Inform me the moment one of these aliens comes up with an actual method to this madness. Good luck. Over and out."

Jack shook his head.

"Bye, then."

He continued down the corridor, pulling himself over a toppled pipe and squeezing through a gap where the inner workings of the bulkhead had collapsed inwards. As soon as he emerged, the flashlight of his suit started blinking on and off.

"Oh, come on. Really?"

It belched out its last morsel of light and then died. Darkness engulfed him. The night-vision filters in Jack's helmet failed to adjust. He was blind, unable to tell which way was forwards or backwards, up, down or sideways.

His breaths came quicker, sharper, and more shallow. Visions of suffocation, of drowning, of simply being forgotten forever raced through his mind while his sweaty hands flailed desperately through the water for something, anything to grab onto.

He was going to die down here.

And that's when he saw the tiny red light.

He hadn't noticed it while his flashlight dominated everything in an eerie white glow. It looked like a flare fizzing far at the other end of the corridor. Or perhaps it was a reactor core, exposed from its shielding and ready to blow. He couldn't tell. It probably wasn't safe, he knew that, but it was *something*, a poppy-coloured pinprick on which to focus, and he swam towards it as if it were the only other element in all of existence.

His hands brushed unfamiliar objects; more than once his breath caught in his throat as he thought he bumped into the bloated corpse of a crew member. But he was the only fleshy on board, of course. In the darkness, any automata casualty would be indistinguishable from the plumbing, gas canisters and spare munitions floating around him.

God, he hoped his friends weren't down here.

The red light appeared to spread out as he drew closer. A sub-aquatic oil spill, perhaps? Jack wasn't sure his latest theory held much water, if he pardoned himself the pun. But how was he supposed to how drive core fuel worked? Or somnium, for that matter? His suit could handle heat, but he didn't fancy chancing it on something super-corrosive.

But in the seconds that followed, Jack realised the crimson light only spread across the ceiling, not the doomed corridor that continued to burrow through the *Alnitak* in front of him. His heart skipped a beat. He'd over-complicated his theory, as per usual. If a fuel line had split, the flames would be burning *above* the water.

And fire meant air. And air hopefully meant freedom.

Hopefully.

He just might have to swim through an inferno to reach it.

"Let's see how robust this suit of yours really is, Tuner," he grunted to himself, thrashing through the water all the faster.

A jagged hole in the ceiling was his exit. His gloves protecting his hands from the worst of the twisted metal, Jack grabbed an exposed support rod and pulled himself sharply up towards the red heavens. Already his visibility had improved. The surface of the coolant shimmered in a spider's web of silver.

His helmet broke the water and Jack squinted to protect his eyes from the flames. But there was no fire to blind him. In fact, the way the coolant sloshed against his visor was almost tranquil.

A red light on the wall above his head pulsed angrily. Jack turned away from it and splashed in surprise when he discovered the condemning camera lens of a security bot peering down at him from the ruins of what appeared to be their original transit corridor.

"Organic lifeform detected," it bleated. "Hostile status: unknown. Preparing to engage."

"Hostile?" Jack babbled. "What are you on about? I'm not a—"

Rogan and Tuner came sprinting down the transit corridor behind the security bot. It rotated its head one-hundred-and-eighty degrees to greet them.

"Is this one yours?"

"Yes, thank you," said Rogan, pulling Jack from the water. "We'll take him from here. Bolts, Jack. You look a state. We thought we lost you. Why didn't you activate your mag-boots when the water hit?"

"Adi," he gasped. "Is she...?"

"She's fine," Rogan replied, helping him climb to his feet. "The lower levels took the brunt of the missile. Hangar 22 was untouched. And Tork's crew got the shields operational again shortly after, thank goodness. But we've got to get Max's bomb off this ship as soon as possible."

"I didn't want to leave without you," Tuner said apologetically. "Not while you might still be alive."

"Your suit stopped relaying any vital signs," Rogan explained.

"Yeah, it took a bit of a beating. Flashlight is broken, helmet is... Hold on. You monitor my readouts?"

"Of course! How else would we know you're not falling apart?"

"Whatever." Jack shook his head. "Klik's here. She's with the Mansa armada. And the UEC decided to show up, too."

"Yes, we noticed," said Tuner. "There's a bunch of new reinforcements who've arrived in the past twenty minutes, but the longer this fight goes on the more outnumbered we seem to be…"

Jack let go of Rogan, stumbled forwards, then finally found his feet on solid ground. He nodded half-deliriously towards the way out.

"I suppose we'd better finish this fight quickly, then."

16

BEGIN TO DREAM

The war raged on. The *Adeona* tore out of the *Alnitak* as fast as her thrusters could carry her and found a quiet spot past the furthest outskirts of the battlefield. Given the yield of the payload she carried, they couldn't afford to be too close to anyone else.

And Max's device wasn't the only new addition to the ship. Doon and Kruzer had remained on board after securing the bomb to Adi's cargo bay, reminding Rogan and Tuner that somebody would need to transport it upon reaching the Prymalis flagship. Half a dozen security bots joined them, as did a similar number of smaller, eclectic automata carrying battle rifles who desired a more "hands on" kind of fight.

The longer the battle went on, the closer the flagship came to Kapamentis... as did the planet-scorching battle-ships orbiting it like a genocidal forcefield.

"How the hell are we supposed to get inside that thing?" Jack said from his captain's chair. "It doesn't even seem to have any hangars."

"As if we'd get close enough to fly inside one, anyway," Tuner added despondently. "That battleships are eviscerating anything that gets within a hundred kilometres of it."

"And I'd much rather not get eviscerated," Adi said cheerfully, "if it's all the same to you."

"The only way in and out that I can discern," Rogan said, standing beside the hologram table and studying the crude scans provided by the Ghuk, "is one we're all too familiar with. The front door we used on XO-R15. But I don't see how we're getting through it. It's locked down tight and the shielding must be a dozen metres thick."

"Not the *only* way in or out," Tuner said. "Remember when we escaped their headquarters after blowing up the Archimandrite? The building transported us to a silo a few kilometres over."

"It let us out, yes. But do you think it'll just let us *in?* And from where? I hardly think we can go knocking on random walls of their battleships hoping for a shortcut."

"What about the Ministerium?" Jack asked. "The Prymalis built the council chamber, hence why it plays as fast and loose with conventional physics as that base of theirs. Could we find a backdoor there, do you think?"

"Unlikely." Rogan crossed her arms. "Not if even the Archimandrite didn't use it. And if there *was* a safe way through, don't you think the Prymalis would have invaded Kapamentis on foot by now?"

"Yeah, I suppose you're right." Jack deflated. "I guess we're getting in via the main entrance or we're not getting in at all."

"Not at all, then." Tuner's head sank. "Bolts."

Jack tapped out a rhythm on the arms of his chair. Then he leaned forwards and opened up a direct channel.

"Grand Minister Zsal?" he asked. "Are you up to date with all this?"

"You're still out there? I am surprised. I thought the Prymalis would have specifically hunted you down by now. Yes, my aides keep me informed. What are you after this time, Jack Bishop?"

"We have a bomb that can blow up the flagship, but we need a distraction. A hell of a lot of distractions, actually. Enough to keep all of the Prymalis battleships away from the shield doors at its front. You still carry political weight in this galaxy, regardless of your official position. Can you make it happen?"

A pause while Zsal considered this.

"You're confident you can destroy it?" she eventually replied. "That doing so will save enough lives to offset the cost this distraction might require?"

Jack swallowed and glanced back at Rogan and Tuner. He hadn't considered the lethal ramifications of what he was asking for. Everybody was dying in such vast numbers already, it was hard for him to visualise much difference.

"Yes, I am. The way this battle is going, I think it might be the only way. The Ghuk and the automata already agree, if you can believe it."

"Right. Hold on."

They waited. Far beyond the cockpit windows, a Prymalis battlecruiser punctured a Krolak dreadnought with its ballistic cannon, then set alight as the dreadnought launched two dozen missiles in return. The two ships crashed in a fiery embrace.

"It's done," Zsal said suddenly. "I sent out an executive order, though how many ex-members of the Ministry obey it is another matter entirely. They've no obligation to. But enough might keep the enemy distracted to give you a shot. Good luck. May the gods be with you."

"Grand Minister?" Jack tried to reply but the line was dead. "Zsal, are you there? When are they due to...? How will we...?"

"I suppose it's happening now," Rogan said blankly.

"If it's happening at all," Tuner added.

"Either way," Jack said, grabbing the flight stick, "we'd better get ourselves into position. We can't let anyone's sacrifice be for nothing."

They soared around the outside of the battlefield, barely a flicker of thruster-fire from the perspective of anyone struggling to survive inside. Most of what they encountered was merely the wreckage of earlier fights, forever drifting outwards – the burnt carcasses of attack ships, the spent shells of munitions, the clouds of heavy particles and free-falling propellent. Unseen and unobstructed, the *Adeona* stopped a minute later with her nose pointed at the approaching flagship and her back to the vulnerable lights of Kapamentis.

It was a straight shot.

Or it would have been, if it weren't for all the Prymalis battleships still in their way.

"Come on, people," Jack grunted through gritted teeth. "Get those ships away from the door..."

How many empires would follow orders given to them by the Ministry? How many would even listen to them? It was one thing to defend Kapamentis, the most multicultural planet in the galaxy, from a mutually shared threat. Putting their ships at further risk, potentially even sacrificing them for the sake of some outsider's mad plan, was another thing entirely.

The myriad battles were too chaotic for Jack to tell whether fleets were trying to pull the battleships away from the flagship or if they were simply retreating. And it didn't seem as if there were enough allied forces left to keep every battleship guarding the floating base occupied.

But then, one by one – a Drygg frigate here, then a stocky Alpha Rhoden behemoth there – warships broke off from their respective fleets and began targeting the Prymalis battleships near the front of the flagship. Missiles and torpedoes and railgun rounds coaxed the retaliating enemy away from their positions. Slowly but surely, the shielded entrance grew less guarded.

"They're doing it!" Tuner jumped up and down on his chair. "They're actually opening a way through!"

But the more their target became exposed, the quicker everyone's celebrations trickled to a stop. Jack's face fell.

"Erm, guys? Slight wrinkle in our plan. How in the goddamn galaxy are we supposed to get that bloody door open?"

They all stared at the impenetrable shield wall on the front of the Prymalis flagship.

"We could use Max's bomb," Tuner suggested sarcastically. "That's about the only thing in our arsenal that'll do it."

"And then what?" Jack raised an eyebrow. "What'll we do when we get to the quantum core? Give it a kick?"

"How many torpedoes do you have, Adi?" Rogan asked.

"Not enough to make a dent in that," the *Adeona* replied, "as well you know!"

"Come on, team." Jack groaned. "Let's not get tetchy with each other. Not now. Together we can think of something. Can Tork spare any automata battlecruisers?"

"I wouldn't have thought so," Tuner replied. "They're the ones doing a lot of the distracting..."

Jack sat bolt upright with an idea. He opened comms.

"Admiral Blatch, do you read me? God, please don't make me go through your operator again."

"Mr. Bishop?" The Admiral sounded even more stressed than before. "Tell me you're calling with good news."

"You know you asked me to get back to you when the aliens out here came up with something approaching a proper plan? Well, we've got one. And we need your help."

"Listening."

He quickly explained the situation, then asked, "What sort of weaponry did the UEC bring with them from Earth? I'm talking about the, you know, big stuff."

"Nuclear warheads, Jack? Everything that hadn't decayed beyond use. We had no idea what we'd find out here, or if we'd need them to terraform—"

"How many is the UECS *Invincible* carrying right now?"

"Five. How many do you need?"

Jack eyed the approaching mothership uneasily.

"All of them?"

"Christ Almighty, Bishop. I have my own superiors to whom I answer, you know. I can't just..." She sighed deeply. "Sod it. We lose them if this ship goes down, anyway. I've got your ping. Rerouting the *Invincible* to your position now."

"Humanity's propulsion tech isn't exactly top of the line," Rogan said. "How long will your admiral friend take to reach us?"

Jack bit his bottom lip. Now was the time for realists, not optimists.

"Too long," he replied.

"Need something terminated in a hurry?" a worryingly

familiar voice said over comms. "Call the Crimson Crosshairs."

"What the..." Jack stuttered in disbelief. "Christ! Is there *any* comm channel people aren't listening into?"

"Only the interesting ones," the voice replied. "And I *never* forget a mark."

A collection of private attack ships drew level with the *Adeona*. Jack had never seen any of them before, but he recognised the insignia printed on their hulls. A large eye staring out from behind a circular targeting reticule – these were card-carrying members of the Crimson Crosshairs, all right.

"Hey now. Come on, Ichor. That bounty on my head was highly illegal, and you know it. And I thought we were square after I stole back Ode's whiskey for you."

"Oh, lighten up, Jack," laughed the head of the bounty hunters. "You're too easy to mess with, you know that? Fine, straight to business. You need that flagship busted open. I reckon we can do it for you."

"Yeah? What'll it cost me?"

"Nada. It's on the house. Consider it the guild's contribution to the wider public good."

"Why does it sound like the 'wider public' are gonna end up paying for it later...?"

"You presume there'll even be a later. So what'll it be, Jack? You want our help or not?"

"Of course we want it. Do you really think you have the weaponry to break through?"

"Oh, Jack." Ichor was laughing. "Let's just say we have some *very* unregulated equipment on board. Good thing the Ministry ain't monitoring us anymore, 'coz they'd have a fit."

A high-pitched whine indicated that she'd combined the frequency of Jack's comm channel with one of her own.

"Ladies and gentlemen," Ichor said to her fellow guild members. "On my mark, we hit that mothership with everything we've got. And I mean *everything*."

"Do you know how much that'll set us back?" Jack heard one of her killers-for-hire growl over the radio.

"Ah, take it from the Crosshairs treasury," Ichor replied dismissively. "Just think of how much more we'll make when everyone knows we helped bring this monster down!"

"We've got less than half an hour before that flagship reaches Kapamentis's atmosphere," Rogan said pointedly. "Less if they break through enough of our defences."

"Hey, it's now or never," Jack said to Ichor. "Those Prymalis battleships won't stay distracted for long."

"Look who thinks he's giving the orders now! All right, chumps. You heard the man. Let 'em have it!"

Ichor's ship shot off first, followed shortly by all the others. Jack was hardly surprised to see that assassinations paid well. Even at maximum thrust, the *Adeona* couldn't reach half their speed. He wondered if the bounty hunters could have evaded the Prymalis battleships even without the distraction, but it made no difference. Adi couldn't. And once the flagship was breached, you could bet your last credit those meant to be guarding it would take notice.

"Get ready," Jack said to the others. "Once that entrance is open, we'll only have moments to get inside before anyone notices."

The bounty hunters screeched towards their target, suddenly dove like a flock of falcons, then shot back upwards just as quickly as their descent began. At their closest point, they passed less than fifty metres from the hull of the flagship. Jack didn't know if the massive base had shields, or if the Prymalis thought it even needed them, but if it did the CC's ships must have swept right through.

A dozen ships deployed three times as many missiles and bombs from their undercarriages. They were visible as shimmering pinpricks of metal for only an instant – long enough for the hitmen and women of the Crimson Crosshairs to swiftly vacate the danger zone – before the entire flagship was replaced by a blinding, throbbing sun of nuclear fire encaged by lightning bolts the length of whole asteroids. Even the *Adeona* rocked against the resulting shockwave.

"Holy hell," Jack gasped. "Is there even going to be a flagship left after that?"

The maelstrom raged against itself for a long moment, then suddenly vanished again, sucked inwards as if run in reverse. Jack's heart stopped as it winked out of existence. The explosion hadn't even knocked the flagship off course.

But the entrance – the giant, arched doorway through which the crew had sneaked back when it was a base grounded on XO-R15 – had been blasted wide open. Debris floated through the open wound. Quite a few exposed sectors surrounding the breach looked worse for wear, too.

"They did it!" Tuner screamed, after a moment's shocked silence.

"Go, Adi, go!" Jack relinquished control of the ship. "Get us in there before the Prymalis launch a counter-attack!"

She didn't budge.

"*Before* they launch a counter-attack?" the *Adeona* replied. "I'm afraid it might be a bit late for that..."

Despite the best efforts of those attempting to distract them, the Prymalis battleships turned back to their stationed positions. Not only that, but those not otherwise engaged with allied forces were also moving to protect their mothership. Jack estimated that within a minute the entrance to the flagship would be even more heavily defended than before.

The window of opportunity had been too slight.

They'd missed it.

"Oh, *come on!*" Jack screamed in frustration. "Why can't we catch a bloody break?"

"Maybe we can still slip through unnoticed," Rogan said, hurriedly refreshing scans of the battlefield. "Our allies aren't giving up. With the bigger cruisers keeping them busy, we'll be practically invisible."

"Not with *that* thing coming at us, we won't," Tuner said.

One of the Prymalis battleships hadn't moved to protect the flagship. It was gunning straight for the *Adeona* instead.

"We can't fight it," Jack said, reaching for the flight stick.

"There's no outrunning its cannons, either," Adi replied. "I don't know about the rest of you, but I don't want to die trying to flee."

"Then we aim for its artillery," Tuner said resignedly. "The least we can do is give their next target a better chance of survival."

"Ready, Adi?" Jack asked.

"It's been a pleasure flying you all," the ship replied.

A flash appeared on the battleship's flank. Jack winced as he braced for the colossal round that would splinter the *Adeona* in two. But then a second flash appeared against the Prymalis ship a moment later, and it was then Jack realised the brief light he saw wasn't from the muzzle of some giant alien cannon.

The Prymalis weren't firing at the *Adeona*.

Somebody was firing at *them*.

The UECS *Invincible* trudged into view outside the cockpit windows. The two nukes it launched had left twin craters in the side of the Prymalis battleship – superficial damage, for the most part – and the shells from the turrets on its deck barely scratched the enemy's hull. But the battleship changed its trajectory. The path forward for the *Adeona* was clear.

Clearer, anyway.

"Admiral Blatch," Jack sighed. "You're a literal lifesaver."

The comm channel remained silent. It was understandable, really. If he was commanding a small fleet, he wouldn't bother chatting with him either. He watched in dread as the Prymalis battleship closed the gap to the *Invincible* and bombarded it with a flurry of rockets.

"Bolts alive," Tuner said quietly, his small hands pressed up against the glass of the window. "I hope they're all right..."

Humanity had barely scratched the Space Age when it was forced to flee Earth, and their battlecruisers weren't built for warfare against the galaxy's most advanced species. The *Invincible's* twenty-first century hull fractured and burned. Turrets on its deck were reduced to shrapnel. The ship remained intact – just about – but it was apparent even from inside the *Adeona* that it had no hope of making the trip back to New Terra.

"Goddammit." Jack thumped the arm of his chair. "I told them to stay back and provide support!"

"Erm, actually," Tuner said, gingerly raising his hand, "you just told them to come here..."

A passing Oortilian starship peppered the side of the enemy vessel. The Prymalis battleship pursued it and left the limping *Invincible* to its long, drawn-out death. Escape pods and lifeboat transporters fled from hatches and hangars along its flank.

"Should we help them?" Tuner asked.

"We have our mission," Rogan replied sadly. "Besides, what would we even do?"

"Admiral, do you read me?" Jack tried the comms again. "Are you okay? Do you need rescuing?"

"Negative, Mr. Bishop. This old girl's not finished yet. And correct me if I'm wrong, but we've still got to get you inside that mothership."

"I'm not sure that's happening," Jack replied. "The distraction tactic didn't work. The second we blew open those shield doors, all the enemy battleships went on high alert. We're small, but we're not a stealth ship. They'll be looking for ships like ours trying to get inside."

"And the longer we hesitate," Tuner added, "the more likely the Prymalis find a way to seal it."

Silence from the other end. Jack feared the *Invincible's* bridge had imploded.

"Admiral?"

"Still here, Mr. Bishop. This plan our galactic neigh-bours have put together... this bomb you've got on board... how confident are you that it'll stop this threat for good?"

"Brighter minds than yours or mine are behind it, ma'am," he replied. "It's desperate, and the odds aren't great, but the enemy is minutes from reaching Kapamentis. This is the last chance we're gonna get."

"And if we don't stop them here, sooner or later they'll target New Terra?"

"Almost guaranteed, ma'am. They've tried to wipe humanity out once already. This time they'll finish the job."

Another pause.

"I don't know this galaxy like you do, Jack," she eventu-ally replied. "I haven't sailed on solar winds, haven't met the cosmic community we're here to save. Honestly, I don't know if the rest of it's worth dying for. But humanity's come too far and lost too much to give up now. Just promise me one thing, Jack."

"Yes?"

"When the smoke clears and order gets restored, make sure humanity has a seat at the table."

The *Invincible's* thrusters spluttered back to life. It slowly turned its shattered nose towards the flagship. Jack rose from his seat.

"Erm, Admiral Blatch? What are you doing?"

"Giving you the distraction you need."

———

ADMIRAL BLATCH CUT the comm link. She couldn't afford to be dissuaded. Nor did she want to spend her last moments with Jack Bloody Bishop bleating in her ear.

Had she known how much trouble he'd be back when he volunteered for Everett Reeves's wormhole experiment... well, she would have splashed out for a chimp instead.

Still. The data from his unfortunate 'incident' had led to the Arks successfully making the jump to deep space. Humanity lived on thanks to his sacrifice.

Time to return the favour.

"Is the course set?" she asked one of the few remaining marines on the bridge of the UECS *Invincible*.

"Yes, ma'am. The ship won't autocorrect her trajectory, even if all other systems fail."

"Thank you, Private. Go join the others in the lifeboat. Same goes for the rest of you. That's an order."

The operator rose uneasily from his computer terminal.

"Aren't you coming, ma'am?"

"Not this time." She gave him her most confident smile, like she was choosing to stay behind at a bar rather than a dying ship. "Somebody has to stay behind in case this old girl conks out on us."

The remaining marines gathered in front of her and saluted.

"It's been an honour, ma'am," one of them said.

"The honour was mine. Now hurry, before the last shuttle takes off without you."

They sprinted out through the security door, leaving her alone on the bridge save for the deafening alarm calling for everyone to evacuate. Blatch was tempted to call one of the marines back to switch it off.

Boy, was she glad she ordered that Moscow Mule back at the Spacebar now.

The *Invincible* finished aligning itself with the Prymalis flagship and put every ounce of surviving fuel into its enormous rear thrusters. The bridge shook with the force, and Admiral Blatch grabbed the closest railing to keep from tumbling over the side of her command station.

She laughed to herself. At her age, a fall like that could be lethal.

The enemy battleships near the front of the flagship turned to intercept the *Invincible*. Maybe they sensed what she was up to, maybe they just thought of the *Invincible* as easy prey. It didn't matter so long as they were looking her way.

Admiral Blatch pulled her hand from the railing – studied it as if surprised by its thin skin and bulging veins. She'd had a good life, all things considered. Half of it had been spent in the years before the first solar flare hit Earth. Easy years compared to what came after. Even then, she'd played a part in one of the greatest achievements in human history. Front and centre. One for the history books. She could be happy. She could be *proud*.

The Prymalis flagship grew closer and closer, dominating the view outside the bridge's wide gallery window. Every adjacent battleship hurried to block her path.

The Admiral smiled. It was one hell of a view.

"I can't begin to imagine what humanity does next," she said.

Missiles were launched; hulls were ruptured.

The glass of the gallery swam red and burst inwards.

17

ALLIED ASSAULT

With Prymalis attack ships snapping at her heels, the *Adeona* touched down inside what remained of the flagship's atrium.

She wasn't the first to arrive. Other attack ships and transport shuttles had scrambled for the breach the moment it appeared, a great many of which were shot down by Prymalis battleships before the wreckage of the *Invincible* crashed through the enemy ranks, providing the fresh distraction their side sorely needed. Whether they came in support of Tork's plan or seized the opportunity for a ground attack wherever they could, Jack and the crew were happy to take all the reinforcements they could get.

Adi's landing gear crashed through a shattered terrarium. Her loading ramp was halfway open before she even touched down, her various crew members already waiting at the top of it.

Jack stood to one side as the towering security automata stalked out first, followed by Doon and Kruzer pulling Max's bomb. It was even more cumbersome than before, somehow, the runic orb embedded within a bubbled cluster of experimental nukes. The smaller volunteer automata flooded out while Rogan and Tuner waited anxiously across from him.

"This is it," he said, chucking them each a gun brought from the *Alnitak*. "You two don't need to come, you know. Stay on board the *Adeona* and get out of here while you can."

"Don't be ridiculous." Rogan caught and loaded her rifle.

"Together til the end," Tuner said brightly.

"The same doesn't go for you, Adi," Rogan pointed out. "You'll be too big a target if you stay here. Take off the second we're outside. You'll be more use out there, anyway."

"If I'm gone," Adi asked, "how will you get off this ship after you plant the bomb?"

"We'll figure something out," Tuner replied.

They hurried down the ramp, heads down and shoulders hunched, and took cover behind the crumbling remains of the terrarium. Jack was vaguely aware of gunfire ahead. Rogan waved for Adi to take off.

"Go! Get out of here!"

The *Adeona's* secondary thrusters ignited. She rose, blowing dust and debris over Jack's visor, and turned back towards the breach.

"I've never been happier than with you three on board," she said. "Ever since the Iris, I've been free to be my own ship. I just wanted to say thank you. For everything."

A chunk of granite dislodged itself from the ceiling and smashed to pieces less than a dozen metres from her hull.

"Oh, and Jack?"

"Yeah?"

"It never would have worked out between us, you know."

"Don't make it weird, Adi."

The *Adeona* shot out of the atrium and was instantly lost amongst the dogfights outside.

"She'll be okay," Rogan said, albeit without much conviction.

They all ducked as a crackling beam of energy dissipated across the rubble behind them.

"Will *we?*" Jack asked.

He slowly poked his head above the pile of stone and glass. The atrium was full of troops. Other ships came and went as more reinforcements joined them; one lost control of its thrusters and careened explosively into the far wall. Krolaks and Alpha Rhoden advanced side by side. Fleet-footed Oortilian strike teams slunk from shadow to shadow and Trulljanan lumbered through the fray like craggy bipedal tanks. Bodies erupted into fine mists as the enemy retaliated. A shuttle branded with the Negoti Corporation logo landed not far from Jack's position, and he expected the Ghuk equivalent of a private militia to storm out. Instead a battalion of LX-14s came marching through its doors – the same clockwork soldiers, he expected, who they'd liberated from the Order of the First Diakonos.

"Tork? Can you hear me? The bomb's inside. Tell your ships to deploy all of those replicator drill things they have left."

"Way ahead of you, organic." Jack could hear each pop and wheeze of the old automata's gaskets inside his helmet. "Those two tank-bots relay everything to me, beat for beat. You just concentrate on getting those explosives as close to that core as possible. We'll handle everything out here."

More booms and hisses from Tork's end. The *Alnitak* sounded like it was in bad shape.

"And, ahem, good luck, Jack Bishop. Perhaps not all fleshies are so bad, after all."

Jack turned to Rogan and Tuner.

"Got any ideas on how we get that bomb to the quantum core?"

"I don't think we need any," Tuner said. "Doon and Kruzer are ploughing on without us."

Another glance out of cover showed the two tank-bots, plus the towering security bots and their accompanying automata, patiently dragging Max's device through the war zone. A few of the neighbouring strike forces had noticed the suicidal group and were providing as much covering fire as they could. Doon and Kruzer were blasting everything in sight with their plasma cannons.

"Good grief. Do any of them actually know how to prime the damn thing once they get there?"

The aperture of Rogan's eye-lenses contracted and she shook her head. Jack sighed.

"Then I suppose we'd better get after them..."

Sprinting to the next spot that could charitably be called "safe" – a Drygg shuttle that had overturned in its haphazard landing, killing exactly zero of its power-armoured inhabitants – Jack caught sight of his first Prymalis since leaving XO-R15. His stomach lurched. The combination of obsidian exoskeleton, ruby-red eyes and fanned headdress of spines never ceased to chill his blood, it seemed. He considered firing a shot at it, then changed his mind. It was better not to attract attention. And besides, he wasn't a good enough shot to guarantee he wouldn't acci-dentally hit a friendly reptilian instead.

"How's the bomb doing?"

Rogan stuck her head around the side of the cracked cockpit.

"Hasn't detonated yet. I suppose that's a good sign. We need to keep pushing forward if we hope to catch up with them, though."

"Is there a safe path?" Tuner asked.

"We could follow Doon and Kruzer," Rogan suggested. "The security bots might be able to stroll over anything with those crane-like legs of theirs, but the tank twins are crushing everything they come across. We won't have Krolak ground troops making sure *we* get across in one piece, though."

"That might leave us a bit exposed," Jack replied, "especially if the tanks are flattening everything in their path. What if we stick close to one of the other units pushing forward?"

The closest ground team was a regiment of tiny goblin creatures in miniature mech-suits. A force to be reckoned with, perhaps, but not exactly the ideal group for Jack and the automata to hide behind. A platoon of Luethians were attempting to advance further to their right, no more than a short jog away, but were suffering under the full fury of a Prymalis counter-attack. It was hard to tell how many fighters they'd lost to the erratic disintegration rays, but there were a hell of a lot of spare rifles lying about. Then again – with four arms available, they might have carried two each.

"I say we take our chances with the path the tanks made," Tuner anxiously suggested. "At least it's the quickest and most direct route."

"Agreed," said Jack. "We can always team up with another group along the way if we have to. See that dislodged block over there?"

Rogan and Tuner nodded. One of the cubes that enjoyed randomly rearranging the walls of the Prymalis base and Ministerium headquarters had embedded itself in the atrium floor.

"Don't stop until you reach it. And let's hope it doesn't decide to fly off somewhere of its own accord. Ready?"

Everyone clutched at their rifles.

"Go!"

The block was approximately twenty metres from their position; from the second they left the cover of the crashed shuttle it felt like twenty miles. Scarcely an inch of the vista before them wasn't occupied with explosions, laser fire, mutilated corpses or glimpses of the Prymalis defensive line.

Tuner tripped over an exposed power line and fell. Jack disobeyed his own advice and turned back, grabbed the little guy around the middle and dragged him the rest of the way. Rogan yanked them both into cover.

Green particle beams crackled and fizzed against the other side of their block. Evidently, their crossing hadn't gone unnoticed. And Doon and Kruzer were halfway to the other side of the atrium by now – too far to follow in one go, or to provide any assistance – especially with a number of their own automata escorts having fallen along the way.

Jack popped out with his rifle raised. His reticle found a Prymalis head; he fired three times before darting back into cover too quickly to tell if any of the rounds had hit their target. He waited a few seconds, then leaned out again. The Prymalis was nowhere to be seen.

Rogan and Tuner mirrored his strategy on the other side of the block. If they were any more successful at killing the enemy, they didn't mention it.

Jack spotted another Prymalis soldier skulking towards the reptilians on the far side. Pinned down by forces further ahead, they didn't appear to notice its advance. Remaining in cover, Jack held his breath and tried to keep his hands from shaking as he lined up the shot. Two quick squeezes later and the Prymalis crashed to the floor, twitching. One last shot put the monster down for good.

"How much additional ammunition did you bring?" Rogan asked.

Jack froze in thought.

"Well, none. How much did *you* bring? There wasn't much left in the crate after the other automata kitted themselves out."

"So we're almost empty," Tuner said, inspecting his magazine. "And we're not even close to—"

A dull thud on top of their stone block sent their attention skyward. A Prymalis soldier, its ancient carapace chipped and snapped, screeched down at them in a bloodthirsty rage. Jack raised his rifle in a panic and smacked it against the wall of the block by mistake. The Prymalis lowered its energy weapon...

A figure came screaming down from a dropship above. The Prymalis raised its wide, primeval head just in time to lose it from the rest of its body. Both parts tumbled over the side as their rescuer flicked her blades clean of blood and hopped down.

"Hey, guys." Klik beamed at them. "I *knew* you'd need my help."

Jack caught her in a bear hug before she could protest. She laughed and gave his back a few feeble pats in return. Tuner hopped up and down anxiously.

"You shouldn't have come," Jack said through a relieved smile. "It's, well, dangerous."

"Oh, come on," she said once Jack allowed air back into her lungs. "Did you really think I'd let you have all this fun without me?"

"How in the galaxy did you even get here?" Rogan asked.

Klik pointed a thumb at the Mansa dropship silently hovering a dozen metres above their heads. All around them black-clad Mansa warriors with rifles in their hands and plasma-pikes strapped to their backs descended on anti-gravitational stabilisers.

"Caught a ride with this lot," she said, grinning. "Oh, and we bumped into a few more friends outside..."

A UEC gunship drew level with the Mansa transporter, descended to within a few feet of the ground on its lift fans. The ramp at its rear dropped open with a metallic *clang* and close to fifteen marines came rushing out. Each wore a transparent breathing mask over their face, though Jack had little difficulty in recognising who led one particular fireteam.

"Elizabe—sorry, Ginger? What are *you* doing here?"

"Saving your sorry arse, that's what. Did you really think I could sit back on New Terra with my feet up, knowing the fate of the galaxy rests in *your* hands?"

"That, and we're still assigned to the *Invincible*," Duke added. "Had to come whether we liked it or not."

Jack shook his head and cracked a wry smile.

"Your mother wouldn't like this."

"Oh, shut up. As if you'd bloody know. Now tell me what's going on so we can carry out our orders and get back home."

Jack relayed the plan so far. Saying it out loud, he couldn't help noticing it wasn't a particularly good one.

"So what you need is a diversion," Ginger said, surveilling the battlefield. "Standard flanking manoeuvre, I reckon. Privates Bakshi, Nomura, Taylor-Adams – proceed down the left flank on my mark. Duke and I will cover you, then you us. Rinse and repeat til we reach the crumbling overhang of the ramp, ten o'clock. Got it?"

The three other marines constituting Fireteam Sigma nodded. They didn't seem fazed by their situation – he supposed fighting giant bugs for a year did that to a person. His daughter had grown into quite the leader since New Eden, too. Of course, it had been Sergeant Yates in command of the squad back then.

Jack whistled for Ginger's attention before they could leave.

"Seriously, Ginger. Stay safe. This is a bloodbath."

Ginger rolled her eyes.

"Pfft. Tell me, Jack. Which of us has won a war before?"

Fireteam Sigma advanced to the next point of cover, intermittently shooting at the Prymalis as they went. Klik grinned.

"She's cool. Hard to believe she's your spawn."

"Please don't ever phrase it like that again. Just be ready to move on their signal."

"And what *is* their signal, Jack?" Rogan asked.

Jack thought on this.

"When they start shooting, I guess."

"They're already shooting," Tuner pointed out.

"Then I guess we should probably move. See that crater over there?"

Everybody nodded.

"Run."

Emerald lightning bolts cut jagged paths around them as they sprinted out from behind the fallen block. The Mansa troopers returned fire with rifles that eviscerated everything their rounds touched. Flesh, stone, metal – it didn't matter. Jack felt one of the enemy's lasers crackle only feet from him; the hairs on his head seemed to almost stand on end from the electrical charge. Something exploded nearby, and Jack found himself thrown forwards into the cold, hard floor. He didn't feel the impact, didn't look to see if he was injured. Scrambling back to his feet, he ignored the carnage to either side of him and didn't stop running until he was deep inside the crater with the others.

"So far so good," he gasped. "Any sign of Sigma?"

"They just reached the spot where that big staircase we climbed has collapsed," Klik said, squinting over the top of their hole. "Ginger is safe," she added in a hurry. "They all are, I think."

A rocket went off nearby. Jack winced as pebbles cascaded over his helmet.

"Bloody hell. I'm not cut out for this. How far to Max's bomb?"

Tuner poked his head out.

"Twenty, twenty-five metres, maybe? They've stopped against the far wall for some reason. Well, I assume they have. There's a big fallen pillar in the way."

"Then how can you tell they're there?"

"One of Doon's cannons is sticking out the side," Tuner replied. "And given that we're still alive, I have to assume the bomb hasn't been shot too badly either."

"Anything between us and them?" Klik asked.

"Except a load of Prymalis?" Tuner shook his head. "Nope. Straight shot. No cover and nothing to block our way."

"I can't believe that a lone human fireteam will be enough to distract every last Prymalis soldier," Jack said, "but hopefully enough of them will be pinned down that they don't bother worrying about the only group in the atrium *not* shooting at them. You three good with that?"

"I suppose we'll have to be," Rogan replied. "It's not as if we have any better odds of survival if we head the other way."

Jack nervously inched his eyes over the jagged edge of the crater. He found the spot Klik mentioned with the partially collapsed staircase. There was no sign of Sigma.

"Wait for it... wait for it..."

After what felt like eternity, the five marines rose from behind the rubble and opened fire on the Prymalis clustered in the centre of the atrium. Jack couldn't tell which was Ginger. In his desperation to know she was safe, it took him half a second to remember why the fireteam were putting themselves at risk in the first place.

"Go!"

They clambered back out of the crater, Klik easily making the leap and Jack's boots slipping through the loose granite as if it were sand. The two automata – Tuner carried in Rogan's arms – were almost ten metres ahead by the time he got to solid ground. Jack swore under his breath. Sigma could only provide covering fire for so long. If he didn't hurry, he'd be left out in the open when the Prymalis rose their ugly heads again.

Knowing that to stop and aim his rifle would only slow him down further, he concentrated on following the trail of mild ruin left in the tank bots' wake. Klik overtook Rogan, covering the twenty-something metres in a flash. Jack felt a wave of relief as the automata disappeared behind the pillar, too.

An arc of deadly static struck a decorative half-wall to his left. Jack kept running. The pillar seemed only an outstretched arm away. Klik stood to one side of it, frantically waving him over.

A second beam zigzagged so close to his visor that its polycarbonate screen seemed to bubble, as if it were melting before his eyes. Jack stopped in his tracks, panicking, itching to pull off his helmet before the energy could disintegrate the rest of him. Then he ascertained its intended target – a Mansa trooper who'd been charging alongside him. Even the Empire's high-tech suits couldn't save the soldier from transforming into stardust.

Jack forced himself to keep running despite the shock, reached the fallen pillar, and desperately threw himself over the top of it just as a third beam splashed inches from his legs.

"Am I alive?" he babbled to the rest of the group. "Somebody tell me that I'm still alive!"

"I believe so, for all the good it'll do you." Rogan grabbed his hand and pulled him back onto his feet. "We've hit a dead end."

Both Doon and Kruzer were present, as was the cluster of bombs, though Jack didn't much like the fresh scorch marks and bullet-grooves decorating their casings. Some of the wiring hung loose. Two of the crane-like security bots had also survived the crossing, but the rest of their automata entourage had either perished or chosen to occupy other positions along the way.

But aside from occasionally shooting back at the enemy, nobody was doing very much.

"What's the hold-up?" Jack asked.

"Scans indicate the quantum core lies on the other side of this wall," said one of the security bots. "However, we have failed to determine a means of accessing it."

"Tried blowing it open," one of the tank bots grunted. "Didn't work."

Jack ran his hand against the impenetrable wall. The blocks weren't budging. In fact, every cube in the atrium appeared uncharacteristically steadfast.

"Goddammit. The layout's random. We should have predicted this. There's no way we're getting through."

Tuner tugged at the sleeve of his spacesuit.

"Remember the last time we were here? We desperately needed a way out after I blew up the Archimandrite, and the building showed us one. Maybe we just need to concentrate really hard on where we want to go."

"Concentrate?" Jack ducked as a projectile pinged off the stone wall above his head. "In this place? I'll be lucky to—"

The blocks rearranged themselves to carve a red-lit corridor through the monolithic grey barrier.

"It's easier to clear your mind when you can cache unnecessary data," Tuner said cheekily.

Jack barked out a deranged laugh and slapped Tuner on the back.

"Doon, Kruzer – get that bomb inside before anyone thinks too hard about a bloody sandwich, or something. You two," he said, pointing at the pair of security bots, "stay here and make sure nobody follows."

"Affirmative."

The two tank-bots dragged the cluster of explosives into the tunnel. It was just wide enough for the pair to rumble along side-by-side. Jack hurriedly followed, though not before first ushering Rogan, Klik and Tuner inside.

The corridor seemed to stretch on ad infinitum. Nothing lay ahead of them and, when Jack glanced back over his shoulder to make sure the Prymalis weren't following them, nothing lay behind. The rat-a-tat of bullets and thunderclaps of explosions grew more and more muted until nothing accompanied them but the echo of their group's own gears and footsteps.

"But it *doesn't* go on forever," Jack muttered to himself.

"It's just a trick, a manipulation. You can only stretch space-time so far before it snaps..."

"Hey, I think I see it." Tuner tugged at Jack's hand, encouraging him to open his eyes again. "Well, I see *something*, at least...."

True enough, when he raised his head Jack saw a cube of brilliantly white light at the end of the corridor. The way back remained an impossibly great distance away, though the walk could have lasted no more than thirty seconds.

Doon and Kruzer rolled into the vast spherical chamber beyond with their plasma cannons raised. Jack tensed in anticipation of a shootout that never came. Nobody waited for them. Not only that, but the chamber appeared to possess no entrances of any kind, save for the one through which they presently emerged.

Occupying most of its centre, and kept from rolling over by a network of taut cables hooked into the surrounding walls, was a ginormous black, metallic orb covered in an intricate lattice of what resembled neon purple canals. It emitted a faint, ethereal hum like a soprano singing an eternal high-C.

"For a core that's supposed to be quantum," Jack mumbled in awe, "that sure is very big. Will A.M.I.'s setup do the trick?"

"Oh, you bet it will," Tuner replied. "It might be big, but it's extremely volatile. The perfect catalyst, even with all that casing around it. I could chuck a single plasma grenade and boom – history."

"You two best be careful with that thing," Jack quickly said to the twin tanks dragging the bomb into position.

The cluster was laid at the foot of the core, which barely brushed the floor at its narrowest point. Tuner waddled forwards, reattached some of the wires that had been shot loose, and plugged one his digits into the small, badly scratched interface strapped to its front.

Jack was reluctant to get too close. He'd never asked Tuner how much gamma radiation his suit could keep out. He gently guided Klik to a safer distance and tried opening comms.

"Tork, do you read me? The bomb is in position. Are you there?"

No response. Jack supposed the quantum core was interfering with the signal somehow. They'd just have to hope that A.M.I.'s replicator drills had been attached to enough Prymalis battleships since they last spoke... and that any allied forces surrounding the flagship would have enough time to get outside of the bomb's blast range.

Jack turned back to the group, did a double-take. They were missing a couple of members.

"Hey, where are you two going?"

"Our mission was to deliver the bomb, not blow up with it," said Doon. They trundled back towards the battle on their tank treads with their plasma cannons raised.

"We may not be smart," Kruzer added. "But we are not *stupid*."

Tuner shrugged and turned back to the bomb.

"They're better off helping everyone outside, anyway. Now, let me see how this thing works..."

"Tork didn't explain?" Jack asked in exasperation.

"Oh, he did," Rogan answered. "Which is precisely why Tuner needs to go over everything himself. That doddery old bolt-bucket's instructions would have us disarming the blasted thing."

"The timer activates an electromagnetic relay," the little automata recited to himself, "which in turn simultaneously opens Max's device to ready the neurotoxin *and* arms the nukes. And then the apex—"

Tuner paused and tilted his head, troubled.

"Huh. The last part's missing a binary switch trigger... but that means... oh no..."

He looked up at everyone with a pair of sad LED eyes.

"Someone's gonna have to stay behind."

18

STAY BEHIND

Jack paced back and forth, clenching and unclenching his fists. Everybody else stood perfectly still as if afraid the slightest movement might be interpreted as volunteering. Nobody said a word.

"Well it goes without saying that Klik won't be staying behind," Jack eventually declared.

"What?" Klik flared her mandibles. "Why does it go without... Actually, you know what?" She threw up her hands. "I'm fine with that. I didn't really want to die on this cruddy ship anyway."

"Tuner." Exasperated, Jack gestured towards his small friend. "Go over why we can't just set the timer and leg it out of here again, won't you? There's got to be a way around this."

"I'll keep this as simple as I can," Tuner replied impatiently. This wasn't his first attempt at an explanation. "This bomb is missing a bit. A really *important* bit. Nothing will go off without it."

"Okay. Sure. Did it fall off, or something? Can you fashion some sort of replacement?"

"If it fell off – or got shot off, more likely," Tuner said as one of the less important wires fell loose again, "it'll be back out there in the active war zone. What do you plan on doing, search every inch of rubble for a component you won't recognise?" He shook his head. "And no, I can't just 'make a new one'. Where would I find the parts?"

"What if we don't use the nukes?" Klik asked. "We could just deploy Max's device. With all the Prymalis inside the flagship dead, we'll only have to contend with their battleships."

"The battleships are the real problem," Rogan sighed. "They're the ones glassing our planets and annihilating our fleets. The main reason for blowing up the flagship is to carry Max's neurotoxin to every other enemy ship. If we have to destroy all the Prymalis battleships the old fashioned way – which I fear our combined forces lack the strength to do – then we may as well do the same to the flagship, too."

"So it's A.M.I. and Tork's plan," said Jack, "or we lose, basically. This is our last and only shot. We do this or the galaxy falls."

"I think it was always going to be this way," Tuner said mournfully. "Even if the bomb was set up properly, we couldn't have just initiated the timer and escaped. Something else would go wrong, or the Prymalis would find the device and space it out an airlock. Let's face it. One of us always needed to stay behind to make sure it went off."

Jack grew frustrated. He pointed angrily at the corridor that led back to the battlefield.

"Why the hell can't Doon or Kruzer do it? They were built for war, weren't they? Getting blown up is part of the job!"

"Ha! Do *you* want to go tell them that? Besides, they don't even have any hands."

"So? They've got plasma cannons, don't they? They could bypass the trigger completely and just shoot the damn thing!"

"Another great reason not to make them angry," Klik muttered. "Two great reasons each, actually."

"It should be me who stays," Rogan decided.

"What?" Klik grabbed her metal shoulder. "No!"

"It should be me," Rogan repeated firmly. "I'm the oldest. I've experienced dozens of lifetimes. In a way, I'd be sacrificing the least."

"Oh, nonsense." Jack crossed his arms. "You're scarcely a day over nine hundred. Your best years are still ahead of you. There's no way I'm letting you sacrifice that brilliant supercomputer brain of yours for the sake of holding down a damn switch. You're worth two of me."

"Two?" Klik scoffed in an awkward attempt at inserting brevity to the sombre situation. "Try three."

"I guess we know why Max didn't take you to XO-R15 with him," Tuner said sheepishly. "Judging by the way everything's set up, I don't think his device could be triggered remotely either. Not if A.M.I. chose to incorporate a binary switch trigger into its design. It wasn't that Max didn't trust you, or didn't want you by his side. He must have always known it was a one-way trip. That's why the crew he took was so small. He didn't want the same fate for you."

"And he wouldn't want it for you this time, either," Jack said. "You're not dying here, Rogan. Not after everything else you've been through. I'll do it."

"Don't be an idiot, Jack."

"I'm not!" He took a second to calm himself. "I'm not. Look. Klik has got a whole life ahead of her in which to shake up Mansa and Krettelian society. You and Tuner only escaped captivity a little over a year ago – you deserve to enjoy being free, if only for five bloody minutes! Do you realise how great a life I've had? I was married to my best friend for years before everything fell apart back on Earth. I saw the world, and now I've seen the galaxy. All in all, I think I've had it pretty damn good.

"But Amber... she's gone. Even now, it haunts me. Do you really think I can live with losing any one of you, too? And... well... what exactly would I be living *for*? I don't mean that in a depressed way," he hurriedly added, noticing Rogan's downcast expression. "I'm not suicidal. I don't *want* to die, guys. But this feels like the end of the road. Once we stop the Prymalis – once I've put to rest another one of my crusades, as Amber would have said – there's nowhere left for my story to go. And if it ends making sure the three of you get away safely, well, I think I can live with that. So to speak."

Rogan, Tuner and Klik stared at him in silence. Jack suddenly found it hard to swallow. It was settled, then. He was the one to stay behind.

And now the decision had been made, he felt fine with it.

Better than fine, actually.

Happy.

"And what if the diodic membrane over-oscillates?" Tuner asked casually.

"Erm, what?"

"The tertiary ideate synchroniser. What if it snaps an ingot?"

"I've no idea if you're even saying words right now."

"Exactly." Tuner turned to the others. "Jack *is* an idiot. That's why he's not staying. I am."

"You've got a screw loose," Rogan replied. "Of course *you're* not staying."

"Yeah." Jack crossed his arms. "Who's being the idiot now?"

"For bolt's sake, why won't you take me seriously?" Tuner shouted defiantly. "I've been around for longer than you, Jack. Or Klik. But you treat me like I'm a child just because I'm small!"

"Come on, Tuner. We don't have time—"

"No, we don't! So stop arguing with me and actually listen to me for once! I'm the only one who can stay behind and make sure this bomb goes off, and you know it. And not just because I know how it all fits together in case something else goes wrong. Rogan does, too. It makes sense for me to make the sacrifice because I'm the one already living on borrowed time."

"What are you on about?" Klik asked. "Borrowed time. Do you have, like, a virus or something?"

"Of course not," Tuner replied. "As if I'd let my data core get contaminated like that. I died back on Krett, remember? As near as an automata with an intact data core *can* die, I suppose, but that's just the way automata work. It's certainly how a fleshy would see things if every inch of him got crushed by a giant statue, right?"

"But you're not dead," Jack said uncertainly, "and you didn't die. Rogan got you a new body, and then you fashioned a replacement just like the old one. It was just a, you know... a transplant."

"Not every culture looks at death the same way humans do, Jack. I don't know if I can explain it any better than I already have. Sorry. But I was gone that day. My mind went black until Rogan rebooted me. Totally offline. I died, and whether you agree with my definition of it or not is just semantics. I still wouldn't change anything we did leading up to that point, and every minute spent with you three since has been a miracle. But it's time to balance the scales. Please let me do this."

He idly kicked his heel against the floor.

"I've already had my second chance. Now I want all of you to have your second chances, too."

Jack opened his mouth, shut it again, then shook his head numbly.

"I can't..." he eventually babbled.

"I won't let you," Rogan said, tightening her fists.

"You will," Tuner said, "because you know you have to. Because the longer we argue about this, the more people die, and if we don't finish this fight soon there won't be *anyone* left to save."

Klik rushed forward and hugged him.

"I'm sorry," she said as she squeezed him almost hard enough to buckle his chassis. "I'll always remember our time watching shows together."

"Never did I regret Rogan bringing me back to life more," he replied with a cheeky tilt of his head. "Come on, Jack. You next."

Jack sighed deeply, tried and failed to muster a brave smile, then knelt down beside Tuner.

"I'm gonna miss you, buddy. I'd be a corpse floating out in Dark Space if it weren't for you. You believed I was worth saving when nobody else did—"

"Jury's still out on that one," Klik muttered sarcastically.

"—and you're by far the bravest person I've ever known. I'll make sure everybody hears about what you did today."

"You'd better! And please don't be so despondent, Jack. Your Amber sounded like a smart lady. You don't need a reason to live, you silly fleshy. You live to find your reason. So for bolt's sake, keep living."

Tuner waddled up to Rogan and wrapped his arms around her leg.

"Thanks for looking out for me after Charon snatched us. I didn't know anyone else in our sector of the Iris. If it hadn't been for you, the others might have left me behind."

"Oh, nonsense." Rogan hugged him back. "If it hadn't been for *you*, we never would have escaped that horrid place. This galaxy is about to lose its brightest star. Without you, it hardly feels worth saving at all."

"You three are the best friends I've ever had," Tuner said, stepping back towards the bomb. "And Adi, of course. Tell her goodbye from me, will you?"

"Maybe there *is* another way," Rogan said desperately, moving to close the distance between them again. "We just need to figure it out..."

"But there isn't time." Tuner pressed a button on the front of the bomb's interface. "I just started the countdown. If you don't leave and alert the other fleets, they'll all get caught in the blast too."

"Fine," she said. "If you won't go, then I'll stay here with you."

"No, you won't, because that decision isn't the remotest bit logical. I'm your best friend, Rogan. I know you better than you do."

"We've got to get out of here," Jack said to Rogan.

"I won't leave him," she said, securing her metal feet to the floor.

"We don't like this any more than you do," he said as Klik grabbed her other arm, "but there are more lives than just Tuner's at stake. Please, Rogan. We still need you."

Rogan ground the metal plates of her face together,

fixing Tuner with an expression of agonising, aching loss, then spun around and marched towards the exit.

"I've already said my goodbyes once," she groaned as she broke into a jog. "Twice the heartbreak is simply unfair."

Jack glanced over his shoulder as the three of them sprinted out of the quantum core's chamber. Tuner gave him a friendly wave. Jack raised a sorrowful hand in return.

Then the dull grey blocks of the corridor began to close behind them, and moments later, Tuner was gone.

So were the crimson walls, the elasticity of dilated spacetime, and the background pop and grumble of an active battlefield. This time it felt like only a second or two passed inside the corridor before Jack burst back out into the atrium and the great monolithic wall sealed over again.

"Tork, it's Rogan." She delivered the words in conquered monotone. "We only have minutes before the bomb detonates. Tell everyone who'll listen to get as far away from the flagship as they can."

"Erm, yeah, about that." Klik spun in a frantic circle. "How exactly are *we* supposed to do the same?"

Jack clambered up the side of the collapsed pillar for a better look. The atrium was practically empty. A few pockets of Prymalis foot soldiers and allied squads squared off against one another, but the legions of reinforcements who'd flooded the enemy flagship had either died or evacuated. With the Prymalis energy weapons disintegrating most of their victims, there wasn't a lot of evidence to favour one conclusion over the other.

"Hey, Adi?" he said, panic and bile climbing his throat in equal measures. "I don't suppose you fancy picking us up, do you?"

"Way ahead of you, Jack." Dust and debris surged over

the top of the pillar. "Did you really think I'd leave without my crew?"

The *Adeona* descended from a holding position in the dark upper corner of the atrium. A prowling Prymalis turned at the roar of her thrusters and was instantly eviscerated by one of her rotary cannons. She came to a stop with the tip of her open loading ramp hovering a few feet off the ground.

To Jack's enormous relief, Ginger and Duke hurried down to help them up. Klik leaped past them with ease, the metallic weight of Rogan almost sent Ginger tumbling out of the ship, and Jack gladly accepted Duke's outstretched hand.

Also inside the cargo bay were the rest of Fireteam Sigma, an assortment of other human marines, one of the towering security bots and, somehow managing to look slightly ashamed of themselves despite possessing no facial features whatsoever, Doon and Kruzer.

"Where's Tuner?" Adi asked excitedly. "Do we need to wait for him? Because Tork just sent out a call to—"

"He..." Jack lowered his eyes to his boots. "He won't be coming."

"Oh... is he... do we need to...?"

He placed a comforting hand on her girder and said, quietly, "Just fly, Adi. Before we all decide to stay."

"As you say, Captain."

The *Adeona* turned and, with what seemed like only a moment's hesitancy, shot out of the giant breach in the flagship's exterior hull. By this time the ramp was shut tight again, and Jack rushed past everybody gathered inside the bay to climb the stairs to the cockpit, giving Ginger only a cursory nod as he went.

Smaller attack ships continued to hound each other

outside the flagship, and Prymalis battleships clung to its immediate vicinity like limpets. Most friendly warships had already pulled far back, though Jack couldn't help noticing there were even more derelict destroyers and frigates left in their wake than ever before. Their wreckage parted before the relentless flagship with all the resistance of a beaded curtain.

The enemy battleships didn't pursue with any vigour. Jack supposed they believed the remaining allied fleets were cutting their losses and retreating. Even the combined strength of the galaxy wasn't enough to stop the technologically (and in their eyes, biologically) superior Prymalis after all.

The *Adeona* took a winding, strafing but *incredibly* expeditious route away from the enemy's armada in case any of them chanced one last shot at her, and then came to a stop far from the flagship. The Prymalis base was no more than a couple of minutes from breaking into Kapamentis's upmost layer of atmosphere.

Adi kept her skip drive on standby in case something went wrong and they needed to make a quick escape.

"This is our last shot," Jack said by the cockpit windows. "Let's hope it works."

"Yes," Rogan said gravely as she stood beside him. "And let's hope it was worth all it cost."

TUNER STOOD ALONE beside the quantum core and watched the runic symbols on the bomb's interface tick by.

Not long left.

He guessed the Prymalis didn't know he was there. It wasn't as if a lone automata in possession of a rifle almost too big to carry was going to hold back the hordes if anyone came to stop him. They weren't scared, just arrogant.

This was fine with Tuner. After all, the best way to depart this galaxy was not with a whimper, but a bang.

The biggest bang of all, with any luck.

That was something to be proud of, he supposed.

Tuner performed a quick check that the rest of the setup remained operational, that it hadn't lost any more vital components since it was brought into the chamber.

Nope. Everything besides the binary switch trigger was present and in perfect working order. Well, not perfect. *Decent* working order. Smoking, battered and *sparking* working order. The important thing was the cluster of bombs would indeed blow up when they should.

Great...

He'd had a good life. Better than most automata, that was for sure. Even the decades he spent in servitude as a hacker-bot before Charon's Rakletts stole him to build the Iris weren't *that* bad... not compared to how some other automata had it. And how many bolt-buckets like himself got to explore the galaxy as a free citizen? How many got to make *friends*?

He sure would miss them. But he supposed they'd miss him more, given they'd still be alive and all, so when you really thought about it, which of them had it worse?

Tuner jumped as the countdown reached zero. Max's device hissed as its top hemisphere rose an inch and rotated ninety degrees anti-clockwise. The nukes clustered around it beeped once in unison.

It was time.

Tuner brought the tips of three exposed wires within millimetres of one another, then paused. It felt like the situation called for some last words.

He would have smiled if he could.

"Boom!"

———

THE PRYMALIS FLAGSHIP CAVED INWARDS, adopted the shape of an hourglass for a short second, then ceased to exist at all. Even the nukes couldn't inflict that level of destruction – it was the quantum core igniting a miniature supernova. The closest enemy battleships were caught in the blast and destroyed. Those further away turned to flee or engage the retreating allied forces. The twinkling lights of numerous Kapamentis districts blinked out as an electromagnetic pulse washed over the planet.

Particles from Max's neurotoxin, diluted by the flagship's artificial atmosphere, were carried across the cosmic battlefield. The drills plugged into the hulls of almost a hundred surviving Prymalis battleships replicated these traces and pumped fresh payloads into their life support systems.

Those who survived the mission watched all this unfold from the *Adeona's* cockpit windows. Jack's words caught in his throat. Rogan bowed her head and chose to say nothing at all.

"I'm sorry about your friend." Ginger stood behind them.

"Yeah." Jack didn't turn from the glass. "Thanks."

One by one, the Prymalis battleships began to drift aimlessly as the toxin attacked their crews' nervous systems. Of course, the allied forces would be taking no chances. With the enemy disabled, every available fleet would soon close in to finish the job.

A few battleships did manage to skip out of the system, either because the drill attached to them malfunctioned or never picked up any payload or, perhaps, simply because those piloting it managed to trigger the jump before the toxin killed them. It didn't matter. A lone Pymalis ship was still a threat, but now the whole galaxy was on the hunt for renegade survivors.

They were the exterminators now.

"We pretty much just committed genocide," Jack said to Rogan. "I know I said we were left with no other choice, but... does that make it right?"

Rogan looked at him sadly.

"Nothing about this is right, Jack. But it's done. The future of the galaxy, the safety of trillions of lives, is secured."

She pushed past the assorted humans on her way out of the cockpit. Far below them, the lights of Kapamentis gradually flickered back to life.

Yes, the galaxy has a future, Jack thought. *But it's up to us to decide if that future is bright or dark.*

19

A SEAT AT THE TABLE

Ambassadors, dignitaries, emissaries and countless bodyguards and general assistants crowded inside the lobby of the Ministerium. Quite a few representatives present were military leaders who'd survived the battle above Kapamentis, or politicians who'd either accompanied their respective fleets (from a safe distance, of course) or just so happened to be planetside when the attack came.

Thousands more were expected to arrive in the coming hours, sent from across the galaxy on the fastest skip drives their species could provide. For the time being, all discourse was being held in the lobby of the Ministry headquarters rather than the vast Ministerium chamber, apparently to keep any latecomers from thinking the other empires had started proceedings without them. That said, Jack noticed a number of new arrivals emerging from the council chamber itself, and couldn't help wondering if the other doors he saw around its circumference really *did* open up on other secret locales throughout the cosmic community.

He gulped. Had anyone had found the Archimandrite's

body yet? *That* could make for some awkward diplomatic conversations.

Given their pivotal role in ending the Prymalis threat, Jack, Rogan and Klik had been permitted access to the otherwise private gathering. It was an honorary invitation – it wasn't as if they'd be privy to the more complicated political wrangling to be conducted behind closed doors. Still, Jack noticed quite a few curious glances thrown in their direction as they passed through the thick lobby doors.

"Didn't expect to see some of these faces back here so soon," Jack whispered to the others. "There's the Krolak minister. She's chatting with that Alpha Rhoden as if they're old friends. Hell, that Argentian isn't even *trying* to eat those Scrap Rats. What progress we've all made."

"I doubt there's a single species in the galaxy who hasn't had its ego cut down by the Prymalis," Rogan replied. Though still visibly dispirited, she'd brightened slightly in the nine and a half hours since the battle ended.

"Not all of them," Klik said snidely. "There are plenty of empires who didn't send anyone to defend Kapamentis."

"And of those, many because to do so would have meant instant annihilation. But yes, there were some notable absentees. It's a matter I'm sure will be addressed in time. For now we should just be grateful the Ministry is back on its feet again. Not every Prymalis was wiped out by Max's neurotoxin, and there are still others that never attended the battle at all. We'll need a coordinated effort to track down and destroy those that remain."

"No chance of diplomacy, then?" Jack asked. "Not even now, in the aftermath of all these divided species working together?"

"Do you think those craggy bastards would agree to an

armistice?" Klik snorted. "They expected to exterminate all sentient life in the galaxy less than half a cycle ago."

"Even if they did, out of genuine contrition or mere desperation," Rogan added, "could anyone really trust them? It's not as if any of their soldiers could be integrated into our society after the atrocities they've committed. And that's all who's left, I believe – any non-combatants in their population were likely killed when their flagship blew up. Then again, who knows how their caste structure works. We saw them breeding new warriors in tanks, remember?"

"Can't stick them on a backwater reserve world somewhere," Klik said, shaking her head. "They'd only bide their time and rebuild their ranks. Besides, one faction or another would try to get revenge on them eventually."

"So that's it, then?" Jack shrugged. "We take out those that remain and go back to how things were before?"

"Well." Klik snapped her mandibles together. "Not *exactly* like before..."

Tork whirred and wheezed his way out of an assorted mass of less popular dignitaries as soon as he saw them stroll down the lobby's central aisle. Kansas and Kay-13, the automata's official representatives at the Ministry, were still en route from Detri.

"You're here," he whistled and hissed. "Thank goodness. I'd rather hoped not to spend this much time around fleshies again... no offence intended, Jack, I'm sure you understand..."

His lone eye like a Super-8 camera lens studied Rogan's forlorn expression, and the old automata sagged on his rusty, mechanical spider-legs.

"Awful to hear about Tuner. If I had known there was a fault with the device, if there'd been a way to take his place... He was one of our best, Rogan. I'm sorry. He will be honoured, let me assure you."

"Yes, he will," said a muffled, metallic voice.

Grand Minister Zsal stood beside them with all four of her armoured gauntlets clasped together. Her complicated breathing apparatus had made a return, of course. Having seen what lay beneath her mask, Jack was privately glad.

"The whole galaxy will know what your friend did for them," Zsal continued. "And how the automata came to the rescue of organics who have no right to expect such compassion. Thanks to them, and the crew of the *Adeona* in particular, the citizens of countless worlds can return home."

She studied the masses gathered in the lobby.

"If I'm being honest, I never believed I'd see the various empires come together like this again. That we're not all slaughtering each other is a minor miracle in itself."

"A shared goal has a habit of pushing perceived differences to one side," said Philo Na Ji, joining them. "May we not so easily forget how close we came to losing what unites and divides us today." He bowed slightly to the group. "Klik, Jack, Rogan. Glad to see you alive."

"Yes, well, on the topic of changes." Had Zsal been in possession of any eyes, Jack would have bet there were glints in them. "The former Grand Minister and I have been discussing his successor, given his new position as Acting Head of the Mansa Empire. We thought it perhaps a good moment to announce the first Krettelian minister, too."

"A Krettelian? On the Ministry council?" Klik flared her mandibles in alarm. "But an enslaved species can't be represented, can it? You don't mean...?"

"Yes, the Krettelians will have to be emancipated, as we discussed," Philo Na Ji replied with a wry smile. "So unfortunate," he added sarcastically, "but I'm sure my people will come to see how strong the former Empire can regrow when both our species work together."

"Philo Na Ji had one name he'd like to put forward for the job," Zsal said cautiously.

"Yes?" Klik stared at them blankly. "Who?"

Everybody waited for the penny to drop. Jack, smiling, cleared his throat rather deliberately.

"I think she's talking about you, Klik."

"Erm, what? Are you? Why?"

"Can you think of any Krettelian better suited than yourself?" Philo Na Ji replied, quivering a fleshy eyebrow.

"But I'm just a kid... well, not anymore, but... I mean, what do I know about galactic policy? I've been on the run from society since I was born. I've probably broken more laws than I even know about."

"And yet you've fought for the Krettelians' freedom all your life, have you not?" Zsal said. "Who better to fight for their best interests now?"

"Somebody needs to hold my replacement to account," Philo Na Ji added. "Your father was the leader of a local resistance faction, yes? It's in your blood. If you're even half as fierce towards your political opponents as you are me, you'll be unstoppable."

Klik turned to Jack and Rogan and smiled pleadingly.

"Don't look at us," Rogan said kindly. "It's your choice."

"Oh, why the hell not," Klik said, throwing her hands to the air. "I can always quit if I hate it, right?"

"A ministerial attitude if ever I heard one." The Mansa leader gently put his arm around Klik and guided her towards a pocket of purple-clad dignitaries. "Now, if you're to get a head start in your new career, there are a few people you ought to meet..."

"She can handle herself," Rogan whispered to Jack.

"Oh, I know. It's everyone else I'm worried about."

Grand Minister Zsal rested one of her four metal gauntlets on Jack's shoulder as he watched Klik disappear into the crowd. He eyed the hand uncomfortably.

"We shall have to discuss the matter of humanity's seat, as well," she said. "Your species has certainly proven itself a worthy addition to our community, should it still wish to join. Mr. Bishop, would *you* consider the role of minister?"

"Me?" Jack snorted. "No, I don't think so. Wouldn't know where to start, and I'd just step on everybody's toes. Or tentacles. Sorry, is that rude? See, I'm doing it already…"

"Jack." Rogan elbowed him in the ribs. "You're blabbering."

"Politics is not for me," Jack said, "and I wouldn't want to embarrass Klik in her new job. But humanity would be honoured to join, thank you. I'd be more than happy to act as an intermediary, or something. You know, present some suitable candidates."

"Very well. I shall keep you looped into future discussions with the UEC. For the time being, however, you'll have to excuse me. There are quite a few delegates in possession of certain Grand Ministerial aspirations of which they need relieving…"

She elegantly intercepted a spacesuited oxen creature coming through the doors behind them. Jack and Rogan took up an awkward position in the shadow of a pillar out of the way of the central aisle.

"I suppose we'd better mingle, then." Jack shrugged. "Oh, look. They have canapés."

"Careful, Jack. You wouldn't want to accidentally eat an honoured guest."

They did their best to introduce themselves to various

heads of state with mixed results. The new Oortilian representative replacing Grand Minister Heram dismissed them out of hand, the Marteusse entourage claimed not to understand Jack despite their translator chips, and the Luethian minister, for all her pleasantness, seemed oddly keen on comparing human anatomy with her own. Every now and then Jack and Klik would catch each other's eye and share a weary expression. But eventually, even with the aid of strong libations served in helix-shaped flutes, the tedium grew too much. That and the muscles holding up Jack's smile were starting to hurt.

"Do you reckon anyone would notice if we slipped out?" he whispered.

"I highly doubt it," Rogan replied. "These politicians are far more interested in themselves than those who saved their lives. Why?"

"Eh, I dunno." He glanced back at the main doors. "There are a few people I'd rather see."

THEY FOUND their friends lurking at the bottom of the Ministry steps outside. It was what amounted to a dry day on Kapamentis, which meant it was the dead of night and everyone was being subjected to a drizzle instead of a downpour.

Ginger was sitting next to Duke and slicking her wet hair back to keep it falling into her eyes when she spotted Jack and Rogan descending. She rose to greet them.

Their hands were inches away from shaking when Sheni Dupont intercepted Jack with an enormous bear hug.

"You made it," he said through a hearty laugh. "We were sure you'd broken your pipe when that battleship turned on you, you know? And when we heard you were headed into that flagship of theirs, man…"

"Are you sure you don't have any regenerative powers of your own?" Gecki rasped. She grinned, revealing rows of short, sharp teeth. "Surprised all your bits are still attached after pulling a job like that."

"Glad to see you guys made it out in one piece, too," Jack said, smirking as he pried himself free from Sheni's grasp. "You did bring a knife to a gunfight, somewhat."

"We did our bit." Sheni crossed his arms and beamed. "Nobody can say we didn't."

Behind them, Duke cleared his throat.

"Erm, guys? Is everything all right with this one?"

Duke slowly edged away from Alan, who'd hopped onto the concrete shelf beside him. One of the alien's big, watery eyes returned the marine's stare, the other gazed off in the direction of the busy traffic flying overhead. A string of drool hung from the corner of his eternally blissful mouth.

"Oh, yeah." Jack dismissed the issue with a wave. "He's always like that."

"Just ignore him and he'll go away," Gecki advised, scratching her scales. "Not that it's worked for us, mind you."

"Paradoxical magnetism," Alan gurgled, his upturned eyeball rolling in a circle.

"The guy's a green bloody jellybean," Duke said, taking a deep breath as he shook his head. "Thought I'd seen it all…"

Ginger cut in; Sheni stepped aside.

"How's it going in there?" she asked, nodding up towards the main doors of the Ministry building.

"So well that I'm standing out here," Jack replied. "A heavy concentration of pompous self-importance, dangerous aspirations and rampant xenophobia. You know, the usual. Glad to see everyone's back to their old selves."

"It's strangely reassuring to see everyone causing problems together again," Rogan added sagely.

"I didn't think you'd hang around for so long," Jack continued. "You two thinking of asking for some shore leave to see the sights of Kapamentis?"

"This place?" Ginger laughed. "Are you kidding? Reminds me of home, and not in a good way. I spent too long hiding from the sun back on Earth to take my vacation on a planet permanently stuck at night."

"Plus there are *way* too many weird aliens for my liking," Duke said. "No offence," he quickly added for the sake of the extra-terrestrials present.

"Lots taken," Gecki rasped. "But I get it. I'd be freaked out by everyone else if I looked as boring as you, too."

"I reckon *we'll* stay a while though, right?" Sheni nudged his reptilian friend in her side. "We're bound to get a few free drinks for saving the planet, you know? And hey – with everyone flying back home now the danger's gone, we might catch wind of a new job or two..."

"Fine, whatever." Gecki growled resentfully. "Xotl says we need to get the *Silver Hart* fixed up before our next flight anyway. And for a ship like that, repairs don't come cheap..."

"What about you, Jack?" Ginger went back to leaning against the concrete shelf beside the steps. "Mission's over. Galaxy's saved. Humanity's gone from extinct to endangered to, you know, vulnerable or something. You gonna jet off to the stars in search of the next planet to rescue?"

Jack ran his hands up his face and through his hair. After so long spent stuffed into his space suit, he actually liked the way the dirty rain felt against his skin. The air tasted smokey and faintly of garbage, but at least that way he knew it was real.

"You know, I haven't really thought about it. I didn't expect to survive this far. By all accounts, I probably shouldn't have." He remembered Tuner's sacrifice, glanced across at Rogan, shared a mournful smile with her. "I think... I think we might be all adventured out. For the time being."

Rogan nodded in agreement.

"In all the time we've known each other, fighting first for our freedom and then against one set of lunatics after another, we haven't had much time to just be ourselves."

"Actually, Ginger," Jack said, brightening slightly, "I might steal your idea, if that's all right?"

"Depends what the idea is," she replied cautiously.

"Back on New Eden, didn't you tell me you wanted to disappear into the wilderness and build a log cabin or something once your term in the UEC was up? The more I consider it, the better something quiet and secluded sounds."

"Eh, you're welcome to it. I'd sooner stick to human civilisation these days. Fought hard enough for it, after all."

Duke cleared his throat to get Ginger's attention. She slapped her thighs and rose from her seat.

"Right, we'd better be off. The *Constellation's* sending a transport shuttle down for us specially. After surviving all this, I don't fancy getting court-martialled for being late."

"That goes for us, too," Gecki grumbled as she grabbed Alan's spindly arm to keep him from wandering into the street. "The leaving bit, that is. Not the getting shot part."

Everybody said their farewells. Sheni shook Jack's hand enthusiastically and then disappeared into the Kapamentis crowds with the rest of his crew. The two visiting humans paused at the bottom of the steps one last time before heading for their assigned landing zone.

"Aren't you going back in there?" Ginger asked.

Jack glanced over his shoulder at the Ministry headquarters, then shook his head.

"Nah, I shouldn't think so. Whatever happens next, wherever our journey takes us along the way... it's time we set a course for home."

20

HOME

FOUR MONTHS LATER

The soft yellow sun bled through the slats in the window. Jack squinted under the hand that shielded his eyes, smiled, and hurriedly closed the blinds. He'd visited countless stars since leaving Earth and couldn't remember once fearing the light they bestowed upon the planets in their systems. But there was something about New Terra's sun that reminded him of home and all the death and disease Sol had wrought.

It also caused him to recall memories of better times, simpler times, before the first solar flares had hit. When exploring the world, not the galaxy, felt paramount. If he closed his eyes and listened for the sound of birds singing from the trees, he could almost believe none of the past two years had even happened.

It had, though. And despite all the heartbreaking loss and agonising hardship and more brushes with death than Jack cared to count, deep down he was glad.

He crossed to the sink and poured himself a glass of

water. Not a bottle, or a rusty tin mug, but a proper glass of water poured from an actual tap. For something so mundanely human, he sure was having trouble getting used to it.

"You would have loved it here, Amber. The rest of you, eh, maybe not so much."

Four photographs hung in frames nailed to the wall. It was anachronistic, he knew, but even though he could access the same images from his data pad there was something special about having them on display. It required effort. It showed love and reverence and thought. More so than swiping a plastic screen, at any rate.

One was of Amber – her passport picture taken not long before the flares hit, a handful of years before he was flung through the wormhole, never to see her again. He had access to photos she took later in life, but he wanted to remember her, well... how he remembered her. Young, healthy, happy. Time could be a messy thing, and to Jack she'd still only been gone a couple of years.

Beside her was a picture of Tuner sourced from Rogan's photographic memory bank. It showed him perched on top of one of the terminals in the *Adeona's* cockpit. Jack thought he looked cheerful. Given their lack of facial expressions, it was remarkably difficult to tell the mood of a lot of automata once you reduced them to a still image.

Over to the right of these memorials were two women who were very much still alive. Klik gave him a thumbs up from the steps of the Ministerium where she worked and Ginger looked dead into the camera in an old personnel file photo that desperately needed updating. One was blood, the other felt more like family. Their pictures were on the wall either way, even if both of them would probably punch his lights out if they knew.

There came a knock at the door. Jack almost choked on his drink. He'd expected company, just not quite so early in the bloody morning.

He opened it to find Rogan standing on the other side with a crate in her hands. He stepped aside to let her in. She set the crate down on the nearest counter.

"Supplies," she said matter-of-factly. "Tinned kwagua berries, some Bursaagu beers, that sort of thing. Couldn't bear the idea of you having to survive off purely human sustenance."

"How very thoughtful of you."

"Are you settling in okay?" Rogan studied the inside of his house as if it were her first time seeing it. "How was your first night on your own?"

Once Jack had decided he wanted to settle somewhere on New Terra, he very quickly came to the realisation that he hadn't any of the skills required to put a house together. Even a shed was outside of his limited abilities (he'd tried). Luckily, a load of automata rescued from the Iris project volunteered to put one together for him based on files from the UEC archives. Aesthetically speaking, it was a log cabin, but it was fitted with luxuries and amenities humanity didn't even know they needed yet.

Rogan had set off to Kapamentis on an errand the previous afternoon, finally leaving him alone. With the generously stuffed crate threatening to crash right through his countertop, he now understood why.

"It was fine," Jack replied. "Took a while to fall asleep. Not used to being somewhere so damn silent at night. I didn't get attacked by any forest monsters, though, so overall I consider that a win."

"Hmm, well. You've got your rifle over the door in case New Terra's last roach comes to eat you. I do wish you'd chosen a plot slightly closer to human civilisation, though."

"I'm not *that* remote," Jack laughed. "It's only a half hour drive to New London. And the way they're expanding the city, I'll have property developers knocking on my door before I know it."

"All right." Rogan smiled. "Well, you know Adi and I are only a comm link away. Tork doesn't anticipate needing us for too long in Detri, anyway. We should be back by... what do you humans call it, again? Ah, yes. Friday."

Jack chuckled and pursed his lips to keep from grinning too hard.

"I'm looking forward to it."

"Sorry to rush," she said, gesturing to the open door, "but we'd best be on our way. Need to stop off in the Haldeir system for supplies en route. There's no point in opening a Visitor Centre on Detri if the tourists have nowhere to eat or sleep, though apparently nobody told Tork that. Wave us off?"

Jack followed Rogan outside. Adi was parked next to the solar-powered light utility vehicle lent to him by the UEC in a dusty clearing flanked by lush fields of grass on one side and a dark wood on the other. The ship let off an excited burst from one of her air thrusters in acknowledgement as Rogan made the climb into her cargo bay.

Jack raised a hand in farewell.

"Until Friday," he shouted.

Rogan waved back as the loading ramp closed. The *Adeona* slowly rotated to face north, ignited her thrusters with enough gusto to blow the leaves off Jack's roof, and then shot off into the rosy sky. First she became a speck, and then she was gone.

Jack leaned against the pillar of his porch, crossed his

arms and watched as the lethargic sun broke free of the horizon to begin a fresh New Terran day.

Jack smiled.

He had a feeling it was going to be a good one.

Thank you for reading!

The *Final Dawn* series may be over, but there are plenty more stories set in the *Dark Star Panorama* universe.

To start with, check out *War for New Terra* – the story of how Fireteam Sigma and the rest of the UEC colonised humanity's new homeworld.

There are lots of exciting books on the way, including standalone novels and series featuring new (and maybe a few returning) characters. To keep up to date on my latest releases (and where you can buy them), bookmark the website below.

www.twmashford.com

Thank you again for supporting the *Final Dawn* series – I hope you enjoyed reading the books even half as much as I did writing them.

– Tom

BOOKS BY T.W.M. ASHFORD

Books in the Dark Star Panorama universe

Final Dawn Series

- The Final Dawn
- Thief of Stars
- A Dark Horizon
- The New World
- The Tin Soldiers
- Ghost of the Father
- The Stellar Abyss
- The Edge of Night
- The Fatal Dark

War for New Terra Series

- Sigma
- Iron Nest
- Royal Blood

WANT AN EXCLUSIVE FINAL DAWN STORY?

Building a relationship with my readers is one of the best things about writing. Every now and then I send out newsletters with details on new releases, special offers and other bits of news relating to my books.

And if you sign up to the mailing list I'll even send you a **FREE** copy of *Before the Dawn*, an exclusive prequel story set immediately before *The Final Dawn*.

Not bad, eh?

Sign up today at www.twmashford.com.

Enjoy this book? You can make a big difference.

Reviews are the most powerful tool in my arsenal when it comes to getting attention for my books. As an indie author, I don't have quite the same financial muscle as a New York publisher. But what I *do* have is something even more effective:

A committed and loyal bunch of readers.

Honest reviews of my books help bring them to the attention of other readers.

If you've enjoyed this book I would be very grateful if you could spend just five minutes leaving a review (it can be as short as you like) on the book's Amazon page.

Thank you very much.

ABOUT THE AUTHOR

Tom Ashford lives just outside London, England with his wife Jenny and extremely needy cat, Kathleen.

An avid movie buff and video game addict, Tom loves all things science fiction. That's why he started the *Dark Star Panorama* – a shared universe full of epic spacefaring stories including the *Final Dawn* and *War for New Terra* series.

His favourite authors are Terry Pratchett and Stephen King.

Send him an email at tom@twmashford.com. He'll enjoy the attention.

facebook.com/TWMAshford
instagram.com/ashfordtom

Printed in Great Britain
by Amazon